The last time Jackie French was bored was 3 December 1967, and she made sure it never happened again. One thing that keeps her from getting bored is her passion for writing.

Jackie French wrote her first collection of short stories, *Rain Stones*, living in a shed with a wallaby called Fred, a black snake called Charlie and a wombat called Smudge. She has since written many books for all ages. The shed is now a house and the animals mostly stay outside!

Hopefully, this book will ensure you are never bored either …

Find out lots more about Jackie French and her books at the following website:

www.ozemail.com.au/~jackiefrench

The Book of Challenges

JACKIE FRENCH

Angus&Robertson
An imprint of HarperCollins*Publishers*

To all the people who organise stuff for kids,
and make a difference

Angus&Robertson
An imprint of HarperCollins*Publishers*, Australia

First published in Australia in 2000
by HarperCollins*Publishers* Pty Limited
ACN 009 913 517
A member of HarperCollins*Publishers* (Australia) Pty Limited Group
http://www.harpercollins.com.au

HarperCollins*Publishers*
25 Ryde Road, Pymble, Sydney, NSW 2073, Australia
31 View Road, Glenfield, Auckland 10, New Zealand
77–85 Fulham Palace Road, London W6 8JB, United Kingdom
Hazelton Lanes, 55 Avenue Road, Suite 2900, Toronto, Ontario M5R 3L2
and 1995 Markham Road, Scarborough, Ontario M1B 5M8, Canada
10 East 53rd Street, New York NY 10022, USA

National Library of Australia Cataloguing-in-Publication data:

French, Jackie.
The book of challenges.
ISBN 0 207 19746 6.
1. Creative thinking. 2. Active learning. I. Title.
153.42

Printed in Australia by Griffin Press Pty Ltd on 79gsm Bulky Paperback

7 6 5 4 3 2 1   00 01 02 03

CONTENTS

INTRODUCTION

Humans aren't meant to be bored.

When animals are bored, or shut up for too long in small spaces, they go crazy — they fight each other, start tearing at their own fur, walk round and round in small circles, groom incessantly, eat or sleep too much or too little (this is more or less what bored people do too) and humans need a heck of a lot more than animals to keep us interested and fulfilled.

A few thousand years ago boredom wasn't a problem. Being eaten by a sabre-toothed tiger, or attacked by the people in the next valley, or finding breakfast was a problem — but not boredom.

Humans have always been good at finding challenges and conquering them. From taming fire to going to the moon, we humans can say 'Been there, done that. Now what?'

Finding challenges — and meeting them — is one of the things that makes us human.

Nowadays it's too easy to settle back and not do anything in particular — to watch TV or play a video game or just hang around talking. Okay, I've got nothing against hanging around and talking — it's one of my favourite activities, and I even like the odd bit of TV (although I'm not so keen on video games — but that may be because I'm lousy at them). Yet there has to be a lot more to life than any of these.

Humans NEED challenges. Challenge makes you feel alive — and the harder the challenge, the more alive you feel afterwards. And the more you achieve each time, the more you'll achieve the next — even if your next challenge is completely different from the last.

I'm bored!

People who say 'I'm bored' are boring. Of course they're boring — they're not doing anything interesting. But if you're bored it's not necessarily your fault.

I was bored most of my childhood. The bits of school I was interested in were too easy; the other bits I hated — and they were even more boring. I loved reading but there were never enough books around; I loved writing but there was no one I could talk to about writing; the bush was something the highway to the beach went through, and there was no way I could get my dad to stop the car and let me explore it.

I wish there'd been a book like this when I was a kid. Hopefully, you can use this book to find some of the things that ARE available. It may not be your fault if you're bored — but it is your fault if you don't do something about it.

Life should be as rich as a Christmas pudding, full of so many ingredients you can't even sort them out. Life should be fun, and sometimes, just very slightly frightening as you think, 'Can I do this? Can I do it? Yes, of course, I can!'

Good luck!

ONE WAY TO USE THIS BOOK

➤ Make a list of five projects you are interested in, and get some of your friends to make a list too. Then compare notes and see which ones you would like to do together. (New things are often easier to do if you have a friend or two along!)

WHAT SORT OF CHALLENGES?

Different people like different challenges. When I was younger (thinner, fitter) I liked plunging down 90 metre drops into dark caves, or wriggling down wombat burrows.

Nowadays, mooching (slowly) to the top of a largish hill is about as physically challenged as I like to get. But for me, writing a book so that it is as good as I can get it (although never quite as good as it should be!) is one of the greatest challenges I know.

For my son it's climbing a mountain — high and dangerous. For my mum it's convincing the government to change its opinion on something she thinks is wrong — or maybe parachuting, which she hasn't got round to yet. (My mum is only 72 and she says she's still got a lot of challenges to cover.)

Some of the challenges in this book may make you yawn or think, 'Anyone who does that is crazy!' No, they're not crazy. They're just challenged by different things.

I've tried to include all sorts of challenges in this book, so if you open one page and go 'yuck', try another … and another … and another. I promise, as long as you're not a jellyfish disguised as a human, there'll be something here to interest you!

NOTE:
Prices and activities given are current at time of printing only and may change at any time.

WARNING

Always discuss any of the projects that you are planning from this book with your parents or guardians, and with as many sensible adults as you can get hold of as well.

Always remember — dangerous things are a lot less dangerous if you do them properly, and things that aren't dangerous at all can be deadly if they are done by a ning-nong with soggy cereal for brains.

Also, don't be impatient. The older you get, the more challenges you'll find — if you want them.

Some adults never really look for challenges at all. They put up with jobs that they are bored with, TV shows they are almost bored with, holidays that weren't quite as much fun as they had expected, even though they cost a lot of money . . .

If you learn to love challenge, and find out now how much more you can achieve once you really start to challenge yourself, I promise you an infinitely more fulfilling life when adulthood finally arrives.

WARNING TO PARENTS AND TEACHERS

It would be an impossible task to check the qualifications and background of the people in each organisation mentioned in this book — especially as many of the groups are voluntary, and membership and leadership frequently changes.

It has to be up to you to check the experience, background and qualifications of anyone leading workshops and expeditions that your kids might be interested in — and to give your kid the guidance they need.

PHYSICAL CHALLENGES

ORGANISED SPORT

The WOW factor

Okay, most sport isn't incredibly 'wow' unless you're really into it, but it is usually fun — a sort of challenge hiccup instead of an explosion.

What does it involve?

Well, that depends on the sport. Some involve two or three afternoons of training a week, or even more, plus regular matches. Other sports are more 'let's get together and have fun on Saturday afternoon'.

How do you go about it?

The first place to ask is your school. Whoever takes you for sport will probably know what sport clubs there are in your area.

The next place to search is the *Yellow Pages*. Look up 'Organisations — Sporting'. There'll be the standard football, netball, hockey, cricket ... but there may also be some you've never thought of; like boule, bowling, gymnastics, fishing, triathlon and cycling.

Most, if not all, of these clubs will be for adults but if you give them a ring, they'll be able to tell you if there are any junior clubs in that sport, or if there are any matches or training. (Most people involved enough in sport to be President or Secretary of their association will be really sympathetic and enthusiastic if you say you're interested in their sport too. Chances are that they'll do all they can to help you.)

> NOTE:
> *The references in the* Yellow Pages *can vary from area to area. So if you look up something like 'Organisations — Sporting' and there's nothing there, think what other category might have been used instead ... look up 'Clubs' or 'Sport' or 'Recreation'. Actually, you can stumble across all kinds of stuff once you start browsing.*

What will it cost?

From almost nothing, i.e. the clothes you are standing in and a nominal amount ($2 or $3) for the hire of a venue, to way on up into the stratosphere. Equipment can cost an enormous amount, (check out the prices of custom-made, carbon fibre framed bikes or handmade fly rods — just for fun!) as can the 'right' clothes and accessories. The thing to remember, though, is to keep it all in some sort of proportion.

If your interest is mild (or possibly fleeting) do not spend a fortune. Instead, check out second-hand and opportunity shops, read the *Trading Post* magazine and keep an eye on community notice boards for bargains in your chosen sporting field.

If, on the other hand, most of your waking life is going to be spent pursuing your chosen sport, then a bit of extravagance can be allowed to creep in! (Just make sure you give everyone a very detailed list of what you want for your birthday, Christmas, and instead of eggs at Easter!)

PACKAGED ADVENTURE HOLIDAYS

The WOW factor

You can abseil down cliffs; jump out of planes (and hope your parachute works); paddle your sea kayak from island to island through the surf; bounce on a raft through rocks and white water; ride your mountain bike through genuine mountains (not just over jumps in the park); ride horses through forests and camp at night … and it will all be organised for you!

Who would be interested?

Anyone who likes active, exciting stuff, is reasonably fit, and has enough money to pay for it all.

What you will be doing

Experienced guides and instructors will take you through the whole process.

How do you go about it?

Look up 'Adventure Holidays' in the *Yellow Pages*. Be prepared to ring up a few companies to compare what's offered. Also ring the State Tourist Bureaus (look up 'Tourism' in the *Yellow Pages*). Explain to the operator what you're looking for, and they'll be able to give you some names. Then ring up the company and ask them to send you some brochures.

Many resorts also offer 'Kids Clubs'. These vary enormously — some are little more than vaguely supervised swimming and games. However, others have fully qualified instructors who'll teach you the basics of lots of activities such as abseiling or rock climbing and have you crawling down the walls of the resort.

So, if you see the words 'Kids Club' or 'Activities for Kids' in a brochure, it's worthwhile finding out EXACTLY what they involve and whether part of your group will be made up of three year olds who only want to make sandcastles. But some resort packages are really great.

Age limits

Some adventure holiday companies won't accept unaccompanied kids; others will, so just make sure you tell the company when you make your first enquiries whether any adults will be coming too.

What it will cost?

Ah, that's the problem — most adventure holidays cost at least $100 a day — and some a lot more, depending on the number of people needed to guide you, and the equipment and transport you'll need.

If you're keen on one of these holidays, it's worthwhile doing a few sums — sometimes you could take the whole family camping AND buy your own kayak for the price of a professionally organised kayaking holiday or a holiday at a resort that offers windsurfing and the like.

Danger level

Minor injuries like a few bruises, blisters and bumps can be expected on most adventure holidays; more major ones (like broken arms, legs or death) are possible. Most companies ask you to fill in a form (called a disclaimer) at the beginning of your holiday saying that you won't sue them if you come back missing a few fingers, half your brain, and so on.

This should give you a clue that severe injuries, while not likely, still happen. Adventure companies must be registered and usually keep to an extremely high standard. But the activities ARE adventure, and with adventure you're never entirely safe. (And sometimes, just sometimes, you find companies that don't follow the rules.)

Where can you go from here?

Most of the staff at an adventure holiday organisation are people who really love doing the stuff and have formed a company so they can do it all the time. Some companies run training courses in white water rafting, abseiling or other activities, and when you reach a certain level you too can be a paid guide, either with that company or another. Or form your own.

If you really enjoy any of the activities ASK the people in charge how they became qualified, how you can get qualified, and where else you can go to do the activities a bit cheaper (i.e. for free).

One of the benefits of these 'Adventure Holidays' is that they give you a taste of the activities, so you can see whether it's worthwhile buying your own equipment, learning more, and joining a club.

Before you go and buy equipment though, it's worth asking yourself whether the thrill of rafting through white water, jumping with a parachute, or sea kayaking will still be there after you've done it twenty times. Is it REALLY something you'll want to do for years, or just every so often?

After you become reasonably proficient in an area, some companies will let you come with them for nothing — not as a guide, but just as an experienced hand to help things along. But all this varies enormously — depending on the activity and who's running it, but at least ASK. As I said, nearly everyone employed in these activities are there because they love it. (In some cases 'fanatic' might be a more accurate description.) Almost always they'll be able to give you a lot of advice — about two-thirds of which might be really useful. (It's up to you to check if what you're told is true, won't kill you, and is really worth trying.)

What can it lead to?

Once you're experienced and qualified as a guide, you can be employed by similar companies, either in Australia or overseas — or start your own. Some schools and resorts also employ instructors for outdoor activities.

BUSHWALKING

The WOW factor

Walking through a world that's not human at all — a totally different world from the everyday; sharing the experience of tree and bush scents and animals with people who feel like you do about the bush.

The 'wow' factor also depends on where you bushwalk — I still remember the extraordinary shock of pride the first time I climbed up a mountain in the middle of a National Park — knowing that the only way to get up there was on foot. There were no roads for cars, or even anywhere that a helicopter could land. It was a place only a few people ever saw and I felt incredibly privileged — and very proud — to have made it there.

I also remember the first time I crossed a flooded river by inching my way over a sagging damp rope, with just another wet rope to hold onto. It was quite safe, as long as I didn't slip or panic, if I panicked I could be swept away.

Basically the more you have to push yourself — physically or mentally, ('No, of COURSE I won't fall!') the greater the challenge and exhilaration at the end of the day. (But I also remember a lovely gentle walk I had with an elderly friend a few years ago — no strain, no pain, no puffing … just a wonderful day filled with trees and birds and friendship.)

Who would be interested?

There are two sorts of people who love bushwalking: people who love the bush, animals, plants, birds; and those who like to see how fast they can climb a mountain, and gallop sixty kilometres in a day. (Don't worry — there is bushwalking to suit both sorts of people!)

I have a blind friend who bushwalks, and in some National Parks there are boardwalks and other tracks that are suitable for wheelchairs.

What does it involve?

There are many sorts of bushwalks, and most clubs offer walks to suit many different types of people.

There are 'doddles' — gentle strolls up small hills or along level paths, just enjoying the scenery and each other's company. They are the sort of walks you can do if you're elderly or not very fit, or carrying a baby in a backpack. These types of walks can take a couple of hours, or even a short day.

There are also longer walks that take a full day, and these are for people who are reasonably fit, but they are still not too strenuous.

Good, solid walks, where you need to be quite fit are also an option — and you really feel you've accomplished something at the end of the day.

And then there are 'tiger walks', which are for people who really don't care much where they go as long as they do it faster than anyone has ever done it before. (I'm biased — I like walks where I have time to catch my breath and have a look at the plants and animals around me. Okay, *some* tiger walkers love the stuff around them too!)

Walks can take a few hours or a day, or many days, and you camp each night. These are much more challenging, as you have to carry tents, clothes, food and, in many cases, enough water and food to last you the entire walk. This means you learn to cope with the absolute basics, even measuring out exactly how many squares of toilet paper you might need so that you don't carry extra things that you don't need around with you.

What sort of walks?

Bushwalks can be along established paths or trails through the bush, or along tracks that can peter out, so you have to have a fairly good sense of direction in order to know where to go next (and a good map), or they can involve walking through country that has no paths at all.

You have to be pretty much a dingbat to get lost on a clear path, but otherwise you do need to learn how to navigate in the bush before you go walking in areas where the paths are not clearly defined.

But while you can probably drag any reasonably sensible adult along with you on a bushwalk with a path, you will need at least one, or preferably two, experienced adults when walking in rougher country. (This is so that if there's an accident one can stay with the injured person while another goes for help.)

There have been a lot of tragedies where inexperienced adults have taken parties of kids for bushwalks and they have been caught by bush fire, floods, or blizzards, or have been lost. Even if you are a kid, it is a good idea to ask the leader of any bushwalk exactly what experience they have had. Good questions you could ask include: Have they done this walk before? How long ago? Do they have a compass and do they know how to use it? Do they have a crepe bandage in case of accident or snake bite?

If they just say 'Duh?' to any of those questions, it would probably be safer to find another leader.

How do you go about it?

Method no. 1. Find a bushwalking club. Look up 'Clubs and Societies' in the phone book and ring up the bushwalking clubs you'll find there. Most reasonably large towns (and many quite small ones) have a bushwalking group.

The clubs will probably be for adults, not kids, but they may have kid's walks too — and they will probably be pretty helpful, and tell you if they know of any other bushwalking clubs that might have junior activities.

The National Parks Associations are adult organisations but if you can coax your tame adult along for a couple of walks, you might then be welcome to go unaccompanied. Kids are usually welcome on most walks when accompanied by a parent, but check before turning up. Each region has their own branch, so consult your *Yellow Pages* for the closest.

Another good place to find out about walks or bushwalking groups is at shops that sell camping equipment. Also, environment centres usually have a list of clubs and societies involved with the bush.

Bushwalking clubs usually send out newsletters listing all the walks that will be on and who to contact if you're interested in going on one of them. The newsletter should also tell you how long the walk will take, how difficult it is, and what sort of terrain there will be — such as mountains or a fairly level path.

Method no. 2. Ask your bookshop or library if they have any books or maps that have good bushwalks in your neighbourhood. Your local National Parks and Wildlife office may also be able to give you good material about bushwalks in your area.

Then persuade some kind-hearted, and reasonably energetic, adult to take you. Some walks may be safe and clear enough for you to do with just your friends and without adult supervision — although this is something your parents or guardians will have to decide — don't just decide to gallop off and do it.

Method no. 3. Police Youth Clubs, Scouts, Venturers and the YMCA run bushwalks. If there are any of these operating in your area, it's worth giving them a ring. You have to be a member of Scouts or Venturers to go on their walks, but the other groups often organise walks that anyone can go on. The people who run the YMCA, Scouts, Venturers and Police Youth Clubs are the sort who will try to organise something if there are a whole bunch of kids yelling that they're interested and want someone to do something about it.

Method no. 4. Form a bushwalking group at school. In other words, see if you can find a mob of kids who would like to go on regular walks. Then all you need to do is find someone qualified to lead the walks, like a teacher or a parent. Or you could ring up your local (adult) bushwalking club and say 'We're a mob of kids who desperately want to go out into the bush but can't find anyone to take us. Help!!!'

Most members of bushwalking clubs will be extremely sympathetic to any poor suffering group of kids who are being sadly deprived of the experience of going bush, and the chances are that you'll be able to find someone who'll take you.

See also the The Duke of Edinburgh Award on page 183.

Walking by yourself

Some people like to walk in a largish group of 10–15; others like to walk with just one or two other people; some people like to walk by themselves. I used to do this — it can be wonderful just to be by yourself in the bush, with no other human influences around you.

But before you do any walk by yourself, you need to be VERY experienced, over 18, and you need to tell someone where you're going and when you'll be back, just in case something happens.

There are an enormous number of things that can go wrong in the bush — from bush fires to breaking your ankle to being bitten by a snake, so it's good to have several years of experience walking with groups before you decide to head off by yourself.

There may well be walks in your area that are okay for you and a few friends to do by yourselves, without any adult supervising you and telling you not to pat the tiger snakes. But this is a matter for you and your parents and guardians to decide.

If you're really keen to do some unsupervised walks, the best bet is to gradually get as much experience as you can so that you can assure your parents that OF COURSE you won't pat the tiger snakes, or walk off the track, or forget to reapply your sunscreen, or light fires. You should also pop down to your local library, look up the walks in your area, and see which ones might be suitable to do alone (i.e. the ones with clearly defined tracks).

Remember too, that it is much safer to go in a group — as long as ALL of you are sensible. (A group is only as sensible as it's dumbest member.)

Age limits

Most bushwalking clubs won't take kids unless they're accompanied by an adult, but if you're really keen, and can persuade an adult to take you the first few times, you may get to know other adults in the bushwalking group who'll be happy to take responsibility for you (with your parents' permission of course!).

Most bushwalkers are generous, friendly people (I'm a bushwalker so I'd know — of course we're all wonderful people!) and you would probably be able to find someone who will let you know when a walk you might be interested in is on.

Be honest with yourself — if you're sure you can keep up with adults and keep going for the entire day — great. But if you get exhausted walking back from the bus, or have had no experience of doing something physical for the entire day, it would be best to stick to a short bushwalk first, so that you can get an idea of what your body is capable of — and get fitter too.

What will it cost?

One of the great things about bushwalking is that you can walk for days, weeks, or even months ... and it doesn't cost a thing except for your food and bootleather.

Once you've had some experience bushwalking it's one of the cheapest forms of adventure around — you just get together a group of bushwalking friends to go with, organise your gear, consult your maps (or the maps at the library), tell someone where you're going and when you'll be back (just in case something happens and you aren't) and off you go.

Most bushwalking clubs have a small membership fee — about $10 or $20 a year to cover costs, though it's higher for some clubs. After that, though, you can go on as many walks as you want to.

But there can be some other costs involved when bushwalking. Firstly, you need to get to where you're going to start walking. Many clubs 'car pool' to their starting point — in other words, you might be able to get a lift with someone else going on the walk who lives near you. Or, in some cases, you may be able to get to good walking country by public transport.

You will also need good boots; thick socks (the sort that help protect you from snakes and blisters); a good hat that will stay on even when it's windy; comfortable pants (avoid tight jeans or anything too loose that might tear when you climb over a log); a day pack to carry your lunch in; a water bottle; a good waterproof jacket; insect repellent; and sunscreen. If you really get into bushwalking, you will probably start collecting a billy, tent, sleeping bag, Swiss army knife, and a whole range of other camping equipment.

Danger level

Low to high, depending on where you walk. Most bushwalking isn't dangerous at all — as long as you dress properly and have a leader who knows where they are going and, more importantly, how to get back.

But if your walk involves climbing, crossing rivers which are possibly flooded, or exploring gullies where there might be flash floods — well, the level of danger goes up accordingly.

And, of course, there are (unfortunately) twits who do things like light fires while there are total fire bans during bush fire season, which can kill themselves and other people.

Where can you go from here?

Bushwalking won't lead you directly to any job, but it will give you valuable experience if you want to be a National Parks Ranger, botanist (studying and learning about plants), or zoologist (studying and learning about animals), or ecologist (researching how plants, animals, and the land interact).

Don't tell anyone I told you this — but it's also a great way to meet people of the opposite sex! I know a lot of people who met the person they ended up marrying on a bushwalk. (Including one kid who met her future stepfather on a walk, and invited him back home to dinner to meet her divorced mum. They fell in love and, well, you can probably fill in what happened next!)

Bushwalks are also a great way to really get to know people, to learn how to be self-reliant, how to pace yourself, when to keep some energy in reserve so you can climb that mountain before it gets dark, and how to keep on going when your body says 'No, I've had enough'.

But for me the best thing about bushwalking is getting to know the bush — a world away from humans.

People talk a lot these days about aliens landing and finding new planets, but most of them don't even know the non-human world beyond the cities and the suburbs, the world of trees and wombats and the small things that burrow into the ground.

CAMPING

The WOW factor

Being away from civilisation, cooking for yourself — and coping without the shelter of a solid roof and four walls — is not quite the same challenge as it was for our ancestors a few thousand years ago, but you are able to get just an echo of it.

Who would be interested?

Anyone who likes the bush or the beach and being independent.

What does it involve?

Camping can be part of bushwalking — you carry a small tent, your food, bedding, and clothes, and set up camp each night in a new place as you walk along. You can also walk to a place that probably won't have anyone else around because you have to WALK there, not drive, and then either stay there in the peace and beauty, or go for day walks and come back to camp each night.

You can also drive to camping grounds — not just ones with caravan parks that can be crowded, but also ones by a beach, river, or lake, or any other beauty spot established in national parks.

It can also be fun just to camp in someone's backyard, the backyard of a holiday house, a friend's farm or bush block, or in a caravan park if your parents are staying in the caravan. You get the fun of being independent — cooking for yourself, sleeping away from the house, not having anyone tell you what time to put the torch out and go to sleep, but the adults are within call if the tent blows down or the vampire from last night's horror movie decides to visit.

How do you go about it?

Try a bit of backyard camping first, in case you get the horrors when the only thing between you and the night is a thin tent wall. Then maybe you can convince your family (you'll know how to do that better than me) to go on a camping holiday.

The great thing about camping holidays is that they are just about the cheapest holiday around — all you have to pay for is the petrol to get there (and in some cases you can even get a bus), camping fees, if any, and of course your food, but you would have been eating that anyway.

Once you've had some experience camping you can be more adventurous. Sometimes we have friends' kids camping on our farm — where they are safe from intruders and can yell (okay, scream pretty loudly) for help, but basically, they are still by themselves.

Last holidays I drove my son and some friends down to an isolated camping spot by a river. They stayed there on their own for three days, cooking for themselves and yarning till 2 a.m. And I was very, very glad to see them safe when I picked them up. But they are all very experienced campers, and between them had certificates in First Aid and Lifesaving (and a mobile phone in case of emergency!). The year before they had camped by themselves in the camping section of a caravan park, while we were more comfortably indoors a little further away. They were still independent, but we were only a few shrieks away.

Scouts, Venturers, Outward Bound and the YMCA all run camping expeditions, often with other activities included. You need to be a member of Scouts or Venturers to go with them, but they'll provide most of the equipment and are a very cheap way of getting a good taste of camping.

Outward Bound and the YMCA run camps that anyone can go on. They cost more than Scouts or Venturers, but generally, are not too expensive. Neither organisation makes a profit, so you'll really just be paying the expenses involved. If you can't afford the cost, it's still worthwhile talking to the organisers in case they can come to some other arrangement about money with you.

See Outward Bound on page 185.

See also the The Duke of Edinburgh Award on page 183.

What will it cost?

Most camping grounds charge about $5–$10 a night —
but in many cases (particularly in national parks)
there's no one there to collect it — check first whether
you need to book and pay for a site in advance. Other
camping places are free. Camping grounds which are
also caravan parks usually have a toilet and shower
block, sometimes they have a canteen where you can
buy basic food and supplies, and often a place under
shelter where you can eat and cook if it rains, possibly
with gas barbeques. Camping grounds in a national
park will have toilets — usually pit or composting
toilets, not flush ones. They may also have a tap — if
you're lucky — as well as fireplaces, but that's all.

You will also need a tent or bivvie bag (a sort of
combination tent and sleeping bag), sleeping bag, torch,
utensils to cook and eat with, and a pack to put
everything in. Often these can be borrowed from family
and friends. Then, if you like camping, you can put them
on your Christmas 'wish list' until you finally get enough
of your own stuff.

Sleeping bags cost anywhere from about $100 to
many hundreds, depending on the type and how much
cold they'll protect you from. (If you need a sleeping
bag but can't buy or borrow one you can make your own
by sewing up a doona into a bag shape, then adding a
drawstring around the top so you can pull it tighter
around your body.) It is possible to do without a sleeping
bag, though, if you don't have to lug your gear very far …
just use ordinary bedding. But a sleeping bag is a great
thing to have anyway — they are really convenient
for sleep-overs and visits to other people's places when
there's likely to be more bodies than beds!

A very basic two-man tent costs $130–$300, but more
sophisticated ones can cost thousands, rather than
hundreds, of dollars. Garage sales are a good place to pick
up small tents — they are often sold when kids have left
home or the family has bought a larger one. But do make

sure that the tent is waterproof, has a ground sheet sewn into the bottom (in case creepy crawlies decide to join you at night) and doesn't show signs of wear at the seams. If it does it will tear into rags with the first big wind!

A bivvie bag costs about $300–$600, although I have seen them on special at the end of the January holidays for under $100. A bivvie bag is a sort of combination tent and sleeping bag. It'll protect you from the dew and the rain, but you don't get the same sense of security you do in a tent, which can actually make sleeping in a bivvie bag very exciting ... you really feel as if you are part of the bush. (And you really are as safe, or as exposed, as you are in a tent — it just doesn't feel that way.)

Bivvie bags are also good when you don't want to have to lug a sleeping bag and a tent over long distances.

Danger level

Low to medium ... staying in a tent is more dangerous than a house — branches can fall on it, you can't lock out intruders, you need to watch out for poisonous spiders and biting ants, and it is much easier to burn yourself badly with a campfire than it is on a kitchen stove.

Where you might go from here?

Camping won't lead to any career I can think of, but it will make you more self reliant and a lot more confident that you can cope with anything (like a tent blowing down in the middle of the night or weird noises at 2 a.m. which might be a zombie or werewolf but is more likely to be a possum after your breakfast or a koala shrieking in the trees).

ABSEILING

The WOW factor

You will zip down a cliff or down a building without a nice safe elevator around you to protect you — sort of like Superman, but with a rope and harness instead of super powers.

Who would be interested?

Anyone who loves a thrill and won't panic. You don't even have to be especially fit.

What does it involve?

There are many places you can abseil which are easy to get to, from cliffs in or near cities, to tall buildings. Also, abseiling is often used by rock climbers, or while canyoning or caving.

Basically, your instructor will help you into your harness and show you how to 'walk' your way down a cliff or wall; the harness stops you falling or going down faster than you feel comfortable with (despite the fact that you're dangling down a cliff, you're really quite safe) and the whole process is really incredibly easy to get the hang of.

That's abseiling. It gets more complicated and a lot more challenging when the cliff bulges in, out and sideways, or if you're plunging down a 90 metre drop into a deep, dark cave with a river at the bottom and a small piece of rock — and you hope it's the rock you're going to land on, not the water ...

How do you go about it?

Abseiling MUST be taught by someone who is qualified. There have been some horrible accidents when twits who have done it once or twice decide to show their friends how it's done.

Abseiling courses are given by rock climbing clubs, caving clubs (see pages 40 and 49), sometimes during

Scouts, Venturers or Outward Bound courses or by Police Youth Clubs (see pages 181–185).

Some adventure holidays will also give you basic or advanced abseiling lessons. Look up 'Adventure Holidays' in the phone book.

Once you learn how to abseil, you'll be ready to take on more dangerous territory — cliffs, canyons, and down deep caves.

What will it cost?

The Paddy Pallin company offers half-day courses from $37 to $59 and full-day courses for $110, but prices will vary a lot between different companies. Usually, the further away from the city you need to go to find a good abseiling spot, the more expensive the course will be because of transport costs.

The cheapest way to learn how to abseil is with Scouts or Venturers, but although the people teaching you will have done a State Government recognised course in abseiling, they are unlikely to be abseiling specialists, or to have done as much abseiling as the instructors in private companies have — but you will learn the basics.

Danger level

Low to very high, depending on where you're abseiling.

Abseiling should be very safe, as long as the harness is used properly, the ropes are checked for fraying and little bits of dirt that can damage them from the inside, and that you wear a helmet, proper boots and clothes, and keep your hair tucked up. (I once saw a girl trapped when her harness caught in her long hair — it was horrible and tragic.)

Abseiling can also lead you into dangerous territory. There's a cliff not far from our farm where several climbers have lost their lives when parts of the cliff above them gave way and fell on them.

But IF you are in safe place; IF you use good quality equipment; IF you do what you are told; IF you don't panic when you find yourself dangling in mid-air; and IF the person teaching you is properly qualified, it is probably less dangerous than crossing the road. (Just a heck of lot scarier.)

Where can you go from here?

You might become an abseiling instructor, though usually you would need to be qualified in other outdoor activities in order to get a job at a holiday resort or with an outdoor adventure company.

Abseiling is also a useful skill if you're going to join the police, fire brigade, armed services, State Emergency Services, National Parks Service, or any other profession where you may have to rescue someone.

PARACHUTING

The WOW factor

You're falling, and the ground is an awfully long way down ...

Who would be interested?

Anyone with a sense of adventure and slight case of insanity. (Okay, I'm biased — and both my son and my mum plan to do it.)

What does it involve?

Your first go at parachuting will involve going up in a ridiculously small plane to an even crazier height, and then jumping out into the sky 'in tandem' i.e. strapped to an instructor. The instructor will be the one who will do the hard stuff, like pulling the cord (in case you freeze with terror), and showing you how to land.

Age limits

You need to be 14 years old or over for a tandem jump, and have your parents' written consent. ('Yes, my son/daughter is crazy enough to want to jump out of a plane and I'm crazy enough to agree.') You will need to be over 18 to learn how to jump by yourself.

How do you go about it?

Look up 'Adventure Holidays' or 'Parachuting' in the *Yellow Pages*.

What will it cost?

Very high — about $300 for a tandem jump on a weekend, although it is generally less than that during the week. The costs are much lower for solo jumps with a club once you are an adult. Many regular adult parachutists belong to a club; although club jump costs vary, they are much less than when you're learning.

Danger level

Not as high as you might think. It's not exactly as safe as joining an embroidery club — and if the whole thing fails you're mud. But most jumps are injury-free. The worst danger is landing badly, with an injury to ankles or knees, but even this is pretty rare.

Where can you go from here?

You can become a parachuting instructor, or join a paratroop regiment in the Army — in the USA trained firefighters parachute out of aircraft into burning areas that vehicles can't get to. Most parachutists, however, just do it for fun!

SURFING

The WOW factor

It's just you and the waves — and sometimes waves can be very big and they never quite do what you expect them to.

Who would be interested?

Just about everyone (except me, I like swimming in freshwater creeks better than salt water — seawater jumps out at me when I'm not looking).

A surfer once told me that he always felt totally alive when he was on his board ... his mind always had to be thinking what the waves would do, and his body had to be continually reacting.

What does it involve?

There are many levels of surfing. There's the paddle-and-dash-back-to-the-beach-if-a-large-wave-comes style of surfing; or there is the bob-and-jump style of surfing, where you just go out into the waves and let them crash around you. There is body surfing, which is where you let the waves take you into shore; and then there is surfing with surfboards, which is what my son calls REAL surfing — where you stand on a board, and the movement of your body guides it across the wave. This kind of surfing can be as simple or as high tech as you like.

How do you go about it?

Find a beach (preferably patrolled by surf lifesavers so that there is someone to yell 'shark' or to haul you out if things go wrong) and dive in. Most people learn how to surf from their friends, or just by watching, and trial and error. (I am assuming here that you already know how to swim; how not to get caught in rips or eaten by sharks, stung by blue bottles or a blue-ringed octopus; and have a reasonable amount of common sense.) Keep an eye on your local newspaper for organised surfing lessons, especially during the school holidays.

Getting there

It's probably easier to coax an adult to go to the beach than anywhere else — even if they don't want to stick their ankles in the water. They can sit under an umbrella and read, or watch for tsunamis (I'm paranoid about tsunamis), or bite their fingernails every time you meet a large wave, or wander along the beach and explore the rocks.

P.S. Don't forget your hat, bottle of water, and waterproof sunscreen (applied every two hours, at least). If you do a lot of surfing a few sunproof garments are a good idea as well. You may not really believe in skin cancer now, but take it from me, once you are my age and the doctor starts slicing off bits of you, you will regret all that sunscreen you forgot to put on!

What will it cost?

Free if you happen to be by the beach; a cheapie styrofoam 'bodyboard' will cost about $20 or less; a really good one about $200; and a second-hand surfboard from $300 upwards.

If you are really into surfing you could consider getting a wet suit, so that you can surf in winter too. You can sometimes pick up cheap second-hand ones — my son got one for $25, but that was a real bargain as he knew the kid who'd grown out of it.

Danger level

Low to deadly, depending on how sensible you are, if the beach is patrolled, and on how many risks you take with rocks, rips, sandbars, stormy weather and large waves. There is also the odd, sometimes deadly, risk from sharks, blue-ringed octopus, schools of bluebottles or jellyfish, and out-of-control surfboards.

Australia has many beach fatalities every year and not all of them are overseas tourists who've never been in the surf before. If you include the danger from skin cancer, the risk is even higher and ... okay, okay, I'll stop nagging about skin cancer.

Where can you go from here?

Professional surfers make their living from the prize money they win at competitions and from advertising companies paying them to say that their products are just wonderful. (Some of the products might be good, but I always distrust companies that pay some celebrity to say their product is great, instead of relying on the quality of the product instead.)

You could also go into surfboard production or hiring, or start a surf coaching school.

LIFE SAVING

The WOW factor

Sun, surf, comradeship ... and the occasional 'wow' heroism when you save someone's life. (It might just be Elle McPherson!).

Who would be interested?

Anyone who likes sun and water; for those that like sun, surf and sand there is surf life saving and for those who like calmer, flatter water, there are different life saving techniques to learn.

What does it involve?

For most people who live near the coast there will be a surf life saving club nearby to join. There are weekly training sessions where you are taught surf safety and rescue techniques. There are certificates to be prepared for and competitions to enter if this takes your fancy. For those who would prefer to learn in a pool, or who don't live near the coast, there is The Royal Life Saving Society. They have a junior club you can join, and like the surf life saving clubs, you will learn to be a better swimmer, along with life saving techniques and general pool safety. There are also competitions that you can enter when you are proficient enough.

How do you go about it?

Surf Life Saving Australia operates in all States. The Head Office, (02) 9597 5588, can help you contact your nearest surf life saving organisation or just make contact with your nearest Surf Club (look it up under 'Clubs' and 'Societies' in the *Yellow Pages*) and enquire about their programmes. You can also check out their website at: http://www.slsa.asn.au for more information about what is involved.

The divisions are Nippers, Juniors and Seniors, and you can sit for various certificates, such as Basic Resuscitation, from the age of ten. The programmes are graduated and Rescue, First Aid, Surf Awareness and

Resuscitation and all are taught at appropriate levels. Again, if you become really involved you can compete within your club, and then progress to inter-club competitions, and even to state and national levels.

The Royal Life Saving Society, Australia, is present in all states and territories so look it up in your local telephone directory. It's essentially an organisation that is in metropolitan and large regional centres and is pool based. The NSW Head Office is contactable on (02) 9879 4699 but try your local swimming club for details of local training and competitions that are available for junior members. You can also look them up on the web at: http://www.rlssa.org.au.

With The Royal Life Saving Society you can train for Bronze, Silver and Gold Life Saving Certificates and some clubs organise competitions. Also, some clubs organise their own systems, rather than being affiliated with the Australia-wide Society.

What will it cost?

Different clubs have different membership fees, just ask at your local club.

Danger level

Low to high — lifeguards have lost their lives saving others and although it happens rarely, the risk is still there.

Where can you go from here?

In the USA there are professional lifeguards; but in Australia they are almost always volunteers, although some resorts now have professional (paid) full-time lifeguards patrolling their beaches and pools. Attendants at pools also need life saving qualifications. These can be an advantage for all jobs that involve caring for kids.

Iron Man Competition

Although it's sponsored by Uncle Toby's, the actual competition is coordinated through surf life saving clubs — as long as the club belongs to something called the Super Series. So anyone who is already involved in the Nippers or Junior sections of their S.L.S.C. can enter.

The Junior Iron Man is open to anyone under 20. Nippers have their own programmes. The cost for entering is free for Nippers who belong to a S.L.S.C. (if some places are not filled then non-members can enter), and in previous years it has been $10 for a Junior; although it may be slightly higher now. It is held at different sites in different states, and you would need to ask your club what the finalised dates would be. In summary, join your local S.L.S.C. and you will be informed of the events, dates, place and eligibility criteria.

LONG-DISTANCE CYCLING

The WOW factor

It's just you, your bike and your muscles — now see just how far you can go. The world also looks quite different on a bike than in a car — you'll see things you never noticed and smell and hear them too.

Who would be interested?

Anyone who is ... or be prepared to get fit!

What does it involve?

Long-distance cycling can involve day trips to some scenic spot and back; or weekend or week-long excursions (or even longer), where you camp out or find other accommodation at night. Again, the longer and harder the trip, the greater the sense of excitement, exhilaration and achievement. Some bicycle clubs also give courses in bike maintenance — which is really useful.

How do you go about it?

Join a cycling club — look up 'Clubs' and 'Societies' in the *Yellow Pages*, or ask at any specialty bike shop; they usually have loads of pamphlets about bicycle clubs, long-distance bicycle rides, races, and other stuff for cycling fanatics.

Most clubs are happy to have junior members — especially if they're accompanied by an enthusiastic adult. Some schools have a cycling group that organises rides (day rides or over-nighters). Also, Police Youth Clubs, Venturers and the YMCA often run day- or week-long bicycling trips.

Many adventure holiday companies offer half-day, full-day or week-long bicycling treks. Prices start at about $70 for a day trip, although overnight expeditions usually cost more per day, as they include accommodation.

I have a pamphlet in front of me about a 15-day, 1100–kilometre ride through the Snowy Mountains,

Gippsland, Southern Highlands of NSW and Mornington Peninsula. A hundred people will be riding, and all food and other logistics will be done for you. The cost is $235 for an adult and $135 for a kid under 16 — but you will have to be accompanied by an adult. There are also long-distance bicycle rides from Brisbane to Sydney and Sydney to Melbourne. Riders cover about 85 km a day — so you'd need to be fit and have stamina, and a sturdy bike with good gears. The organisers provide meals, snacks, camping places, mechanical assistance (backed up with spare parts), maps, a support vehicle, and an extensive ride kit. The organisers of this particular trip are Laidback Cycle Touring, 636 Polding Street, Wetherill Park NSW 2164, although there are several other long-distance cycling tour organisers — the best way to find them is at a cycling club.

Every person I know who has gone on a long-distance ride with a mass of other people has said it was one of the most incredible experiences of their lives. There was wonderful scenery (and you feel you are really part of it, because you are not locked away in a car), fantastic companionship and camaraderie from everyone else — and an extraordinary feeling of achievement at the end! It's also one of the cheapest, challenging holidays you can have!

A good website to start with is the Canberra Pedal Power group's site http://sunsite.au/community/pedalpower. Even though you might not be in their area, they still have lots of stuff you might be interested in, and links to other sites. Also try the Bicycle Federation of Australia's website at http://www.bfa.asn.au/touring for links to different touring events happening in each state, including information on how long they last and how much they cost.

Age limits

Most clubs will expect you to be accompanied by an adult and many excursions will be for adults only, simply because you probably don't have the speed and endurance that an adult cyclist may have. But usually there'll be at least some events that you can join, and the more kids who show an interest, the more such events there are likely to be. Each group will have its own rules. ASK!!!! The adventure holiday companies I contacted said that usually kids need to be at least 10 and accompanied by an adult.

What will it cost?

Free — if you have your own bike and do all the organising yourself.

Membership costs for clubs vary; one Police Youth Club I contacted runs a week-long bike ride for $185 a week. But costs can differ, depending on how much paid supervision is needed, how long you are going for, and if you are going to provide your own food, drink and bicycle.

Danger level

Low as long as you're sensible; extremely high if you're a twit who won't wear a helmet or obey the road rules.

Where can you go from here?

Many people just keep cycling to have fun and keep fit all their lives. Like all incredibly successful sportspeople, champion cyclists can win prizes and get sponsorship deals to promote products.

CANYONING

The WOW factor

Canyons are a hidden world — once you're down there it's like the rest of the planet does not exist. And with most canyons, just to get in and out of them is a challenge in itself.

Who would be interested?

You need to be very fit, with a sense of adventure.

What does it involve?

Usually you abseil down into the canyon, then walk, raft or climb out (or a combination of the three). Some canyons are easier to get into than others, and it's just a rough climb down into them — or even an easy climb down a nearby ridge. Some canyons just have a small damp trickle at the base, others have a great roaring torrent. The steeper and the rougher the climb and the more water there is, the more danger is involved.

How do you go about it?

Some bushwalking groups go canyoning (see page 12). Sometimes caving clubs have canyoning expeditions too. There are also canyoning clubs — see 'Clubs' and 'Societies' in the *Yellow Pages*. You can also ask at shops that sell camping and climbing equipment, they often have useful pamphlets or notice boards that may have contact names or numbers.

What will it cost?

Free — if you know someone who is experienced and willing to take you and if you don't need to hire or buy special equipment. If you go with a club the costs will usually be covered by the club membership fee, although there may be transport costs and equipment hire as well. If you go with an adventure tour group be prepared to pay at least $100 a day.

Danger level

High — you are at risk from lots of things; from falling and getting a few bruises, sprains or broken bones, to snake bites; or even to drowning if water levels in the canyon rise quickly.

Where can you go from here?

Canyoning teaches you self-control and self-discipline because if you don't do everything perfectly, you can be killed. Once you are proficient you can become qualified to lead tour groups and, of course, it's a necessary skill in many rescue operations.

ROCK CLIMBING

The WOW factor

This is perhaps the most skilled and physically challenging sport of all — and the greater the challenge of course, the greater the high at the end. Not only that, it is a sport that will also take you into areas of stunning beauty.

Who would be interested?

Anyone who is very fit, very coordinated and won't panic in potentially deadly situations.

What does it involve?

Going UP, inch by inch, ache by ache; and learning how to get over bulges, around overhangs, into and onto places where you would think no human would ever be able to go without wings.

How do you go about it?

Join a climbing club. Start with the 'beginner' climbs, and work your way up to the more difficult ones from there. Some gyms have indoor climbing walls, where you can learn at least some of the basics — but they will only give you a hint of what the real thing is like. Outward Bound (see page 185), some Police Youth Clubs (see page 184) and Venturers (see page 182) also have basic climbing courses, and can be a good place to start so that you can get a taste of it. Some adventure holiday companies also offer rock climbing, so ring around to find out.

Often groups of like-minded friends will climb together and plan their own expeditions (my cousin has a mob of friends she's been climbing with for years, they go off camping and bushwalking together too) but this is definitely something to aim for when you are older and have had a heck of a lot more experience.

What will it cost?

Club membership varies; and some clubs have equipment that can be borrowed or hired for the climbs.

Danger level

High to extreme.

Where can you go from here?

As Edmund Hillary once said, though I can't remember his exact words: To conquer mountains you need to know them, and to know them you need to know yourself. People who climb mountains tend to have a glow of confidence and capability about them. The harder the climb, the more they look as though they are thinking, 'I've done it, and survived'.

ICE CLIMBING

This is like rock climbing, but even more skilled and dangerous. Ask the information centre in any snow area for companies that teach ice climbing. You'll learn how to walk and climb with crampons and ice axes, and practice crevasse rescues — and don't be surprised if they say you are too young. One company I checked with charges about $600 for a four-day course, with food and snow camping equipment included. They said they would have to be convinced that any kid who wanted to come along was fit and strong enough to cope, and had at least some major rock climbing and snow country experience — and you would also have to have your parent's written permission.

ORIENTEERING

Orienteering is a competitive sport where you find your way to a certain, pre-arranged point (usually in the bush) by using just compass bearings.

The WOW factor

Orienteering is a bit like a more competitive form of bushwalking ... you get the pleasure of being out in the bush — but also the thrill of seeing how fast you can get to the end of the 'walk'.

Who would be interested?

Anyone who loves the bush, is interested in increasing their fitness levels, and enjoys the logical challenge of maps and compasses.

How do you go about it?

Look up 'Clubs' and 'Societies' in the *Yellow Pages* of the phone book, or ask at stores that sell camping equipment. You can also look up the Orienteering Federation of Australia's website at http://www.personal.usyd.edu.au/~markz/oz-o/ofa.html and this site has links to clubs in each state.

Age limit

Most orienteering clubs are for adults and families — if you're interested you'll probably have to get an adult interested too.

What will it cost?

Club memberships are usually pretty low. Membership for the Orienteering Federation of Australia is $20 a year for under 21s and $40 for families.

Danger level

Low.

WHITE WATER RAFTING

The WOW factor

Speed, water, rocks, danger, and an incredible adrenalin rush that can be addictive.

Who would be interested?

You need to be fit, be able not to panic, and be a competent swimmer.

What does it involve?

White water rafting starts at level 1 — a gentle drift along a stream with maybe a few gentle rapids; and you progress up to level 5, which is white, furious water, drops of several metres, possible whirlpools, and real danger.

You can also try white water canoeing and kayaking, zapping down rapids and through gorges.

How do you go about it?

The easiest way to get a taste is to save up for an expedition with a tour operator. Outward Bound, Scouts, Venturers, and possibly Police Youth Clubs will also be able to tell you about any training courses that they have available. Once you get more experienced — and get the equipment — you can go by yourself or with a group of friends, but this is something you will achieve with age and experience.

You can also get a taste — just a taste — by li-loing down rivers and gentle rapids (but only with your parents' permission and adult supervision). Li-los are a heck of a lot cheaper than canoes, but they also have a greater tendency to sink in rough water!

What will it cost?

At least $100 a day, or $280 for a two-day expedition and possibly more — depending on your destination with a tour operator. White water rafting isn't cheap — the equipment is too expensive and you need a high level of supervision — and it often costs a lot just to get to the white water. Once you have your own equipment though, and a reasonable level of experience, cost becomes zilch, except for food, sunscreen, and the like.

Age limit

This will vary depending on the danger level. You'll need to be at least ten for anything more than quiet paddles.

Danger level

Medium to deadly, depending on how white the water is (i.e. how rough and steep the fall) and how careful and well prepared you are and, to some extent, how lucky you are ... even very experienced white water rafters have drowned in unexpected whirlpools.

Where can you go from here?

You might become a professional white water rafting instructor, or operate a tour company, or a photo journalist who specialises in wild, out-of-the-way places and adventure sports.

SEA KAYAKING

The WOW factor

The sea is awfully big, and you and a kayak are awfully small — you will get the sort of contact with the ocean that our ancestors had, without the bulk of a great metal ship between you and it.

Who would be interested?

You need to be fit and a strong swimmer.

What does it involve?

You might take your kayak just for a trip along the coast, out to an island, or from island to island. You will find that the sea is a heck of a lot rougher — even on a calm day — than you imagined.

How do you go about it?

The best place to start is to do a one-day course with a professional (look up 'Adventure Holidays' in the *Yellow Pages*) or join a Venturers group involved in sea kayaking. Police Youth Clubs in coastal areas might be persuaded to organise a sea kayaking course if you are enthusiastic enough.

There are several adventure holiday organisations that offer weekend or week-long sea kayaking treks, including one that goes from island to island on the Great Barrier Reef (call the Queensland Tourist Bureau; find the number in the *White Pages*).

Also, try looking up the NSW Sea Kayak Club on the Internet at: http://www.nswseakayaker.asn.au/articles/others.htm for links to clubs in every state.

What will it cost?

The cost can be from $100 a day and upwards for your initial instruction. If you are really hooked on it after you've had a go, then you can look for a second-hand sea kayak or try to hire one. A sea or 'touring' kayak costs about $1195–$2000 new, and $900–$1500 second-hand. (I don't know how easy it is to hire sea kayaks — I wasn't able to find a place that did, but you may be able to.)

While a kayak is expensive to buy, if you look after it well you will still be able to sell it for a large part of the original purchase price (if you get sick of sea kayaking), but most sea kayakers I've known have either gone on to more challenging adventures or, after many years, have introduced their own kids to sea kayaking.

Once you have the basic equipment, it is a very cheap — and extraordinarily exciting — sport. (Although if you're not into big waves and danger it can also be very peaceful just paddling along the coast looking for a deserted beach to have lunch).

Danger level

Low to medium if you only putter in safe areas during calm weather; incredibly high to deadly if you decide to take your sea kayak across Bass Strait, along dangerous coasts, or out in heavy weather.

Where can you go from here?

You might become a professional sea kayaking instructor, or a professional sea kayaking competitor. There are many competitions — especially overseas — some with quite decent prizes.

CANOEING

The WOW factor

Silent speed (or relaxed puttering) and often incredibly beautiful places. Canoeing is also a great way to get away from hordes of other campers and it is a heck of a lot less work than lugging a pack on your back for the same distance.

Who would be interested?

Anyone reasonably fit — though even if you aren't, you can still enjoy a quiet paddle. Even though you will be wearing life jackets, you also need to be able to swim fairly strongly.

What does it involve?

Canoeing can be a gentle putter on a lake, or an exhausting race up a river, or anything in between.

How do you go about it?

It's probably an idea to do a one-day or half-day course (about $100 a day) to learn the basics. Scouts, Venturers, the YMCA and Outward Bound also run courses and expeditions, and they will probably be cheaper than private companies. Some school camps have canoeing as one of the activities, and it doesn't take long to learn the basics.

See also the The Duke of Edinburgh Award on page 183.

What will it cost?

You can hire a canoe with paddles, life jackets and helmets for two adults and two kids for about $45 a day, or $119 for a week (ask at any place that sells camping equipment or look up 'Adventure Holidays' in the *Yellow Pages*). Bung in a tent, sleeping bags, and cooking stuff, and you have a cheap and exciting holiday for the family — if you can persuade your parents that they really will enjoy it!

Canoes, on average, cost about $950 for a new one, or about $750 second-hand — there is so much demand for second-hand canoes that the price is almost as high as new ones. Kayaks cost about $895–$1395 new, and $395–$1100 second-hand.

Danger level

Low if you are sensible, wear life jackets and work out exactly where you are going and how long it will take to get there — most beginners totally underestimate the time their planned journey will take. Always keep an eye on weather reports.

Where can you go from here?

You might become a professional canoeing instructor or an adventure holiday guide.

CAVING

The WOW factor

Somewhere deep underground there is a whole new world — caves that have never seen the light until humans arrived with their caving lanterns, passages that twist and turn up and then down through the hills with great echoing chambers or tiny cracks that you have to wriggle through on your stomach, trying not to think about the million tonnes of rock above you.

Who would be interested?

You need to be fit, and not scared of the dark or small spaces. Caving is definitely not for twits who like to show off, and who may damage caves by their carelessness or threaten other members of the party by not following procedures exactly.

What does it involve?

To go caving you'll need equipment — overalls, a helmet with a light, gloves, boots, and back up lights. You will also need abseiling equipment if you need to go down long drops — or jumaring equipment if you need to get back up again. (Jumaring — going back up — is a heck of a lot harder than going down!) You will also need to learn safety procedures, caving techniques and how to look after your equipment afterwards. (A bit of grit in a rope may mean it frays and breaks.)

How do you go about it?

The YMCA, Scouts and Venturers offer caving experiences, but these are mostly fairly basic ventures into fairly touristy caves. (On the other hand, you may be lucky and find someone who really knows about caves who is prepared to organise something — but mostly the person who takes you will just be someone's parent who has done enough caving to qualify as a supervisor, but not enough to be an expert, or to be really passionate about caves.)

For more challenging caving, look up 'caving clubs' or 'speleological societies' under 'Clubs' and 'Societies' in the *Yellow Pages* of your local phone book.

Caving clubs are primarily for adults, but most clubs will have some activities for learners which are suitable for kids to do. (Mostly these are organised for the kids of members — even if there is only one every year or two. On the other hand, if you ask and show you are interested, it is more likely that someone will organise something that you can join.) The Australian Speleological Foundation has a great website at http://www.rubens.its.unimelb.edu.au/~pgm/austcave/orglist.html and it has a list of many caving clubs all over the country.

You also need a permit to go into most caves these days (this is to make sure that they are looked after so that other generations can visit them too) and a registered caving club is the best way to get entrance into these caves.

N.B. If any twit offers to take you caving with just a torch or two and without proper helmets, boots etc., tell them to go jump (but not down a cave — they will just pollute it). Caving can be incredibly dangerous if it's not done properly and inexperienced parties can also do major damage to caves. (I used to go caving myself and sadly have seen many parties of kids led by people who didn't know what they were doing. With caving it is worth knowing you have to be wary of overconfident adults!)

The National Parks Service have many of the best cave systems under their jurisdiction and offer guided tours of some chambers led by their rangers. You will also probably learn a lot about caves too ... some of the ranger's talks are great. Call your local National Parks office to find out what caves are near you.

Danger level

Low in touristy caves to extremely dangerous — especially if the caves contain underground rivers or long drops.

Where can you go from here?

To bigger, wilder (and more dangerous) caves as an adult!

A THOUSAND CLUBS AND SOCIETIES

➤ I don't know exactly how many clubs and societies there are in Australia. I don't think anyone has ever counted them.

➤ But if you are interested in anything from keeping bees (apiarists) or snakes (herpetologists) to computers, stamp collecting, breeding dogs, miniature cows, horses, budgies or chooks, doll or teddy bear making, antique farm machinery, miniature railways — there will be a club for it somewhere.

➤ The best place to look is in the *Yellow Pages*, under 'Clubs' and 'Societies' or 'Organisations'.

➤ But if you're into, say, antique farm machinery, or breeding dingoes, you may not find it in your local phone book. So zap off to your nearest Post Office and look up the *Yellow Pages* of other district's phone books too. You may be amazed at what you discover!

P.S. Most of these clubs will be for adults, but most will let you join as long as they don't involve activities that they think you aren't up to.

➤ On the other hand, there are some awfully weird people in the world, and dishonest ones. It's a good idea to let your parents or some other reasonably intelligent adult know what you're doing, just so they can run an experienced eye over it, in case there's something odd going on. (There almost certainly won't be, but it's good to make sure.)

ROLLERBLADING (IN-LINE SKATING)

The WOW factor

Speed and ever-increasing skill; jumps, curves and somersaults . . .

Who would be interested?

Just about anyone with good balance and who doesn't mind speed and spills.

What does it involve?

I don't think there's any kid who doesn't know!

How do you go about it?

First get your gear — including a crash helmet and knee and elbow pads, if you have any sense at all. Then get a friend to show you how, or just experiment until you learn the basics!

The YMCA sometimes runs holiday schools in roller-blading during January if you want to learn some more way-out skills. Ask your local council if they have a special area for rollerblading, with jumps and curves. (And if they don't, and there are enough of you interested, collect a petition to ask them to create one for you!) Check out the Australian Roller and In-line Skating website at http://www.blisreel.com.au/skating/homskate. htm for a huge list of where you can skate in each state and city.

What will it cost?

You will pay from $59 for a very cheap type, to around $800 for a custom-made pair. Second-hand in-line skates start from around $50. As it is mostly kids who rollerblade, and kids grow out of their shoes and rollerblades quickly, there is often really good, second-hand stuff around. You will find it in specialty rollerblading shops (sometimes ski shops sell rollerblading stuff too) and at general second-hand stores or pawn shops.

Danger level

Low to incredibly high ... there are possibly more accidents on in-line skates than any other kid's activity, ranging from crashing out into traffic to broken bones and even long term ankle or knee injuries from too many jumps and heavy impacts! Do wear all safety gear possible ... if someone calls you a dork it might just be because they don't have the safety gear you have, and are embarrassed about it. If your knees or your ankles ache, take notice ... it might be time to stop for a while.

HANG-GLIDING

The WOW factor

There is no engine, no nice plane around you. It's just you and the wind and silent speed across the world ... and a heck of a big drop below you!

Who would be interested?

Anyone who has ever dreamt of being a bird.

What does it involve?

Basically, you have a great big kite above you that keeps you up — well, gently descending anyway. You can hang-glide for mile after mile, with nothing but the whoosh of the air and maybe the lap of the waves below you (many hang-gliders love launching themselves from seaside cliffs).

How do you go about it?

Try a tandem hang-glide first, with an instructor who will show you what to do ... and how to stop yourself from plunging to your death instead of soaring and swooping. Then, if you are hooked, you can really get into it: buy or make a hang-glider, and turn into a giant bird every afternoon. Everyone I know who has done it has said that it is a most extraordinary experience — literally so out of the ordinary it's hard to even describe how wonderful it was.

Age limit

Okay, don't race out the door just yet — you need to be 14 before you can go on a tandem hang-glide with an instructor, and even then you must have your parent's written permission. You can hang-glide solo at 17 (but this may vary from state to state — check first).

What will it cost?

A tandem flight costs about $175 at weekends, or a bit less during the week. If you want to be a solo hang-glider, ten days of lessons costs $1650 (yes, wow!) but you may find some clubs where it costs much less — and of course you may also be lucky enough to find an experienced enthusiast who will teach you for nothing!

I've no idea how much hang-gliders cost to buy — I do know that some people make their own, but you have probably got a few years to find out before you can legally go soaring and swooping on your own.

(Note: while hang-gliding is very expensive to start off, it's a very cheap sport/thrill once you're really into it … it's just you, your hang-glider, and the wind.)

Where can you go from here?

You might become an instructor; or design and make hang-gliders; or even go into ultra-light aeroplanes, which are tiny one- or two-person things in all shapes and designs (most enthusiasts make their own). See also 'Ultra-light Aeroplanes' in the *Yellow Pages*.

FISHING

The WOW factor

Eating what you catch, feeding your entire family and neighbourhood after a good day or just quietly mooching around near rivers, creeks, lagoons, dams, surf, jetties. In fact anywhere where there is water and fish, which is always pretty good.

What is involved?

Well, it depends on what you want to do.

Are you a competitive type? Then join a fishing club, enter fishing competitions, take up competitive fly-fishing or tying, and record everything you catch in a diary (species, time, weight, bait, weather, etc, etc.).

Like to spend time dreaming, wandering along on your own? Just take your gear to the nearest piece of likely water and drop in the baited hook or lure.

Fishing is one of those activities that can be enjoyed at different levels by different people, in groups or by yourself. The real decision you have to make is at what level you want to indulge yourself.

How much will it cost?

From $10 for a hand line and some bait; to $25 for a very cheap rod, line and bait; to many thousands for high-performance game rods (and then there is the cost of boat hire and guides and so on), depending on your level of interest and obsession.

How do I get involved?

Badger your favourite parent or any other adult likely to take you, hang about jetties and piers until someone takes pity on you, or join a fishing club. Your nearest tackle shop will be able to tell you what is available, when they meet and how to join. Also try looking up the Australian National Sport Fishing Association on the

Internet. Their website is at: http://www.ansa.com.au — they will have links to different clubs and you may be able to find one in your area.

Fishing is one of Australia's biggest recreational activities in terms of how many people are involved, and how much money is spent. Check out the licensing laws in your state before heading out to do battle with the wily denizens of the deep (or not so deep). The place where you buy your fishing stuff should be able to tell you if you need a licence to fish in any of the areas you are planning to go.

Where can you go from here?

Most people who get hooked on fishing keep fishing on and off all their lives — it's a great relaxing sport that can take you to wonderful places. But you can make your living in the fishing/tourism industry — acting as a fishing guide, taking people out deep-sea fishing on your boat, selling fishing equipment and giving decent advice to go with it.

SNOW SURVIVAL

Some the ski resort areas offer snow survival programmes run by Search and Rescue which are aimed at keeping the young and adventurous safe. Ask at the visitor information centre at whichever snow region you choose, to see if one is available. (For Mt Hotham's programme call Mt Hotham Ski Patrol on (03) 5759 3550. From what I understand, other areas plan similar schemes which may be operational by the time you read this.)

Also, see Ice-Climbing on page 41.

SKIING AND SNOWBOARDING

The WOW factor

It's fast and cold and the nearest you will get to flying with your feet on the ground. It is a quite different world up there above the snowline.

Who would be interested?

Anyone who is fairly fit and supple.

What does it involve?

There are two forms of skiing — downhill skiing, which is FAAAAST but you have to pay for a lift ticket to get up on top of the mountain so you can ski down it. (Unless you really enjoy clambering up a mountain on skis which are designed to take you rapidly downhill.)

The other form of skiing is 'cross-country'. You use a different type of skis and it is basically like bushwalking though the snow. Unlike downhill skiing, this means you can go to isolated places where the only other tracks on the snow will be wombat prints.

Snowboarding is like skiing, but faster, more out of control and on a board, naturally, not skis. You can hire snowboards, as well as the wet/snow gear to go with them. The visitors centre in snow areas will tell you where you can use them.

How do you go about it?

First, you need to find your snow. Apart from a few freak snow falls, you'll only find snow in Tasmania, Victoria and New South Wales. Look up 'Ski Centres' or 'Tours and Resorts' in the *Yellow Pages*, and call the visitors information centre in any region. They will be able to tell you about places to stay, where to learn and, most importantly, how to get there. (There are buses to most of Australia's ski resorts, if you don't have access to a car and driver.)

Second, you need ski equipment, which can be hired at all ski resorts and nearby towns (although it is much cheaper to hire your equipment before you leave home, rather than relying on finding what you need at the resort shops).

Then you need to learn to ski — all ski resorts have instructors — or, if you know someone who is an experienced skier, they can give you lessons, though if you can afford it, a few basic lessons from a professional teacher are a good idea.

You also need to find somewhere to stay — and it is more expensive to stay near the snow than any other holiday place. The further away from the snow, the cheaper the motels and caravan parks are but then you have to drive or catch a bus to the snow everyday.

It is possible to camp in the snow (see Snow Camping) — I've done it once. But you need a special snow tent, sleeping bag and clothing that will cope with that sort of cold — and a very experienced person to go with. It is incredible fun though — you really are in another world.

The best way to get a taste of skiing is to try it on a school excursion or on an Outward Bound, Scout's, Venturer's or Police Youth Club excursion. They will do all the arranging and the cost will be much, much lower than if you do it by yourself. Some of them also own their own ski lodges, so you get much cheaper accommodation, and it is great fun doing it all with a group.

What will it cost?

Downhill skiing costs a lot once you have counted hiring equipment and waterproof clothes, getting there, staying there and lift tickets to take you to the top of the range so you can ski down again. The cheapest way, if you are organising it yourself is to do it as a package (a weekend skiing, plus lessons, lift tickets and accommodation costs from about $400 upwards). Schools, Police Youth Clubs, the YMCA, Scouts and Venturers often offer much cheaper holidays. (If you passionately want to try skiing, and no one in your town is organising a snow excursion, it is worthwhile contacting the YMCA, or Police Youth Clubs in Canberra or anywhere else near to the snow, to see if you can join one of theirs.)

Cross-country skiing costs much less than downhill skiing — you can hire cross-country skis, poles and boots for about $40 a day and can often pick up quite cheap second-hand cross-country skis. You will need, of course, waterproof and warm clothing. If you don't have it, this can be hired — a good parka or waterproof overalls costs about $17 a day to hire, but of course this all adds to the cost.

Downhill skis cost about $450–$1500 new, or $50–$350 second-hand. Ski boots cost about $300–$700, or $50–$150 second-hand. Cross-country skis cost about $350–$1200 new — they are much harder to find second-hand, although it's possible — mine were second-hand. Ask at stores that sell ski equipment if you are interested in second-hand gear; also look at notices on their notice board; or just hunt through 'to sell' columns in the local paper, the *Trading Post*, and other magazines that specialise in people selling second-hand stuff.

At least one Police Youth Club arranges days at the snow for about $25 for the day.

Danger level

Very high. I stopped skiing after one bung knee, a sprained neck and concussion (I did an unexpected somersault and landed in a partially frozen creek). Downhill skiing is more dangerous than cross-country skiing — except that you are much less likely to become lost or disoriented on a groomed downhill ski run than out in the snow covered Australian high country.

Where can you go from here?

You might become a professional ski instructor (but remember you will only be working the part of the year when there's snow — unless you travel overseas chasing the snow seasons). Skiing is also essential if you volunteer for search and rescue in snow country.

SNOWSHOEING

The WOW factor

If you enjoy bushwalking into isolated places, you will love snowshoeing. You strap on these great, flat things and go out into the most stunning country where the only tracks are yours and the animals', and icicles hang from the trees and the world is white and blue and green. (It is really impossible to describe how beautiful the undisturbed world up above the snowline is.)

What does it involve?

Snowshoeing is much easier than skiing; basically you can head off with very little instruction — but you do need SOME instruction, so don't just hire your stuff and think you can head off. Even if snowshoeing is reasonably easy, there are a lot of dangers up in the snow country — like creeks, hidden under snow, that you can fall into, or blizzards that can descend so fast that you're lost in ten seconds. (This is NOT an exaggeration!). You should never go too far away from yelling-reach of other people, unless you are with someone who knows what they are doing because the weather in the high country can change in an instant from sunny and blue to a white-out.

How do you go about it?

The best way is probably to do a day of snowshoeing with a trained instructor or guide, and then if you adore it, next time you can just hire the equipment and go off by yourself. But 'by yourself' DOESN'T mean just you, or even you and a friend — snowshoeing parties should have at least four people, so that if someone is injured there is someone to stay with them and at least two to go back for help — that way no one is ever by themselves. The best way to choose a course is to ring up the visitor information centre (each snow area has one) and ask for a list of companies that offer snowshoeing. The information centre will also be able to tell you the cheapest places to stay and how to get there.

What will it cost?

A day's snowshoeing with a guide/instructor costs about $54 for an adult or $35 for a child, plus the hire of snowshoes and any other snow gear (like waterproof overalls and a parka). A weekend snowshoeing expedition with accommodation and meals costs about $450 per person.

Once you and your group know what you are doing though, you can go off for a much cheaper day of snowshoeing, with the only cost being hiring the gear.

P.S. You can get a bus and/or train to most of Australia's snow areas — again, ring the information centre to get all the details and to find out about student concessions.

Danger level

Low, if you take the time to learn all the safety aspects of being up in the snow country — such as having the correct clothing, a whistle to call for help, chocolate or other high-energy food to help keep you warm if you have an accident and need to wait for help. The longer the trek, though, the greater the danger level, as you can be caught in a blizzard or 'white-out'. If you are thinking of going on even moderately challenging excursions (either cross-country skiing or snowshoeing) there are courses in snow safety which would be a good investment. If you are going far it is also a good idea to take a hand-held GPS (Geographic Positioning System) monitor, a mobile phone (which don't always work in mountains but then again sometimes they do and you could get lucky) and an emergency rescue beacon.

SNOW CAMPING

The WOW factor

Humans are not meant to survive in ice, so to spend a night or a week in the snow means relying on your skills and your equipment. You will be in a world of isolated magic. Until you've experienced it, no one can even imagine the silence and the sheer alienness of a world covered in snow.

What does it involve?

You will need special snow tents and other equipment — unless you are really doing it the hard way and plan to build a snow cave. Most snow camping is combined with cross-country skiing or snowboarding — it's all part of a week or weekend trek into the snow country. And I promise you, after even a few days in what will feel like a whole new universe, you will think you have been away for months.

For guidelines on how to protect the delicate environment of the high country while snow camping, make sure you have a look at the Department of the Environment's website at http://www.anca.go.au/protecte/alps/codes/snowcode.htm

How do you go about it?

You MUST go snow camping with a qualified instructor. (If you don't at the very best you will be cold and miserable; at the worst you will be dead, or lose the odd few fingers, or foot, to frostbite.) Contact the nearest visitor information centre for a list of companies that offer snow camping. A three day trip should cost you about $450, with everything from meals to equipment included. It's also worth contacting Venturers, Police Youth Clubs, the YMCA and Outward Bound to see if they offer any snow camping adventures.

Danger level

Low to medium, if you are with someone who knows what they are doing; extremely high to almost certainly deadly otherwise. And if the weather turns bad while you are out, the danger level will rise dramatically.

MARTIAL ARTS

The WOW factor

Finding out just what your body can do, and being prepared to defend yourself if you are attacked. (You may find that the more physically confident you become the less likely you are to have to use your skills!)

Who would be interested?

You would need to be tougher (and fitter!) than I am.

What does it involve?

Martial arts range from doing short courses in self-defence, to spending years — if not decades — refining your skills and abilities.

How do you go about it?

There are many private martial arts schools — if you are interested, it's best to get your parents to check them out thoroughly, as some are much better than others. Possibly the best place to start with martial arts, though, are the Police Youth Clubs — look under 'Police Youth Clubs' in the *White Pages* of the phone book. Police Youth Clubs run courses in everything from Aikido to kick boxing, gymnastics, Judo, Jikka, Karate and wrestling. The YMCA (look it up in the *White Pages*) often offer martial arts courses as well.

What will it cost?

This will vary — private classes are generally much more expensive than Police Youth Club ones, although some of the private courses are run as a public service rather than for profit. Police Youth Club and YMCA prices are always pretty low, and remember, if you can't afford them, tell the person in charge — both organisations are very good at making sure that no one is left out just because they haven't got a few dollars.

Danger level

Low to medium, depending on what you choose, but if you decide to go into any of the martial arts professionally, or compete seriously as an amateur, the danger level can rise dramatically. Even if you don't sustain a major injury, repeated head buffeting can affect your intelligence, hearing, and balance. On the other hand, nowadays protective clothing means it's all a lot safer than it used to be. (My son does boxing with a Police Youth Club and yes, sometimes I wish he was interested in embroidery instead, but I have to admit it is a heck of a lot safer than I thought it would be.)

Where can you go from here?

You can become a professional in all areas of martial arts. You may find that these qualifications are useful if you are interested in the defence forces, working as a bodyguard, security guard or joining the police force.

See also: Northern Territory Junior Rangers on page 186.

PISTOL SHOOTING

The WOW factor

Some people — particularly the odd dill-brained male — like anything that makes a loud noise ... and some sick people like the feeling of power that a firearm gives them. (If you need a firearm to make you feel good, you badly need to try some of the other activities in this book — the ones that make YOU powerful, not just power from a bit of metal and gunpowder.)

But many people — including females — enjoy the skill and challenge of becoming more and more accurate at target practise.

Who would be interested?

Pistol shooting isn't playing cowboys and Indians — you need to have patience, as well as a steady hand and a good eye to become any good. It's also a sport that can be done from a wheelchair — and yes, you can try pistol shooting if you wear glasses.

Pistol shooting is a competition-based activity, so you have to be interested in clubs and competitions to find it rewarding.

What does it involve?

Contact your local pistol club for full details, but a typical approach is to attend a seminar (which will outline your responsibilities, costs, instruction and training regimes, Shooter's Licence etc.). You and your parent will then be matched up with an instructor, and after 12 lessons at a pistol range (over 3–6 months) you sit a written exam. Competitions are graded, and can be within your club, between clubs, or at a state, national or international (up to Olympics) level.

Age limits

Children can join a pistol club from the age of 12, but they must have a parent who is prepared to become a member and go through the training at the same time. Until you are 21 you must only use an air-pistol, although this may vary from state to state.

What will it cost?

You have to own your own pistol ($600–$800 second-hand).

The typical club fees are:
Joining per family – $100
Annual for an adult – $200
Annual for an additional adult – $40
Annual for an additional junior – $20

How do you go about it?

You will need to join a pistol club ... there will be one in most cities and country areas. Look up 'Clubs' in the *Yellow Pages* of your phone book, and if you can't find an entry, ask your local police station — all shooters and shooting clubs need to be licensed, and your local police branch should know where the nearest club is.

Danger level

Low for pistol clubs; much higher for other shooting activities. Firearms are only as safe as the hands they are in ... and even with tougher gun control laws, some real ning-nongs can get a licence. (I'm feeling a bit cranky about this — some fool nearly shot me last year.)

Generally, the larger the party of shooters, the more dangerous it is.

Where can you go from here?

Pistol shooting is an Olympic sport; and the ability to shoot well may be an advantage in both the police forces and the defence forces. Professional shooters are also employed in country areas to eradicate feral animals like pigs, goats and foxes (yes, I know you may think they're cute — until you see the devastating effect they have on native animals, birds, and the bush).

P.S. Country kids can get their Junior Shooter's Licence at 12, but they must have a licensed adult with them at all times. They must also have a safe place to shoot where shooting is NECESSARY to control feral animals (not just for fun). You can't get a licence just because you have a few acres and want to blast around. You also need to pass an exam before you can get a Junior Shooter's Licence, to show that you know what you're doing and know how to use your firearm responsibly. Contact your local police station for more details.

GO-KARTING

The WOW factor

It's a noisy, smelly, fast, high-adrenaline activity ... this is a great way to mobilise your father, brother, uncles, etc, into spending time with you. (Of course, if your mum is a rev-head she'll be there too!)

Who would be interested?

If you like speed you'll love go-karting. I hate speed, but I can see the thrill in it too — it really is fun ... and probably the closest you will get to driving until you get your 'L' plates.

What does it involve?

Speed and noise in a small vehicle. Go-karting can be an indoor or outdoor activity, depending on your local facility. Some go-kart tracks organise competitions, others are just for fun. Most go-kart tracks require you to gain a licence (a trip around the track qualifies you).

It's easy enough to get around the track on your first go, but the more you do it, the greater the level of skill you'll get. You can really tell the difference between someone who's just beginning and someone who knows what they're doing. As with everything, some people have a lot more talent than others.

Height limit

You must be a minimum of 140cm tall to be allowed to drive yourself (although some tracks have double buggies that adults can take smaller children around the track in).

What will it cost?

You hire the go-kart in blocks of time (10 minutes, 20 minutes or half an hour are typical) for between $10 and $27 approximately. You can go with a bunch of friends and get a group booking discount at most tracks.

Helmets are provided, and you must wear covered shoes (no thongs or sandals).

How do you go about it?

Look up 'Go-karts' in the index of the *Yellow Pages* of your local phone book.

Risk factor

It is much safer than it looks or feels, so it is a great way of experiencing an adrenaline rush in (relative) safety.

Where can you go from here?

Drag-racing, or racing the whole caboodle of cars, bikes etc.; making your own go-kart; or becoming a go-kart builder and designer, or operator.

SAILING

The WOW factor

Well, if you like sailing, there are few things that compare to its pleasures of wind, water, romance, exhilaration and freedom. If you don't, then it is a purgatory of wetness, cold and, sometimes, terror!

What does it involve?

Sailing can be as simple as puttering about in a boat on a calm lake — or as challenging as sailing around the world single-handed.

How do you go about it?

If your parents and/or their friends are into sailing, then you will no doubt already either be involved, or be resisting involvement, but for the rest read on. If you don't have access to a largish amount of water, fresh or salt, forget it. But for those within cooee of lakes, dams, harbours, or the sea, there will, in all probability, be a local sailing club.

Look up 'Sailing Clubs' in your local *Yellow Pages* index and start from there. The YMCA and the Sea Scouts are also possibilities in some areas, as are various outdoor activity groups but a sailing club is a good place to start. If they aren't providing exactly what you want, there will be someone there who will know where to go and who to ask.

What will it cost?

A typical sailing club will have provisions for junior members (who can be as young as seven) and many of them do not require you to bring along an adult. The club will provide tuition and tests (both theory and practical) for juniors. They also provide lifejackets, and access to a fleet of training boats for those without their own, and usually provide storage for boats and gear for those who become boat owners (for an additional charge).

Typical costs for a yearly membership in a fairly basic and modest sailing club (membership in the most flash and desirable clubs would require your parents to take out a mortgage — and they may, possibly, object) are as follows:

Family – $90
Senior – $60
Intermediate – $25
Junior – $15
Social – $30

Where can you go from here?

Well, where do you want to go? Sydney to Hobart? (Although the rules for ocean racing have just raised the minimum age to 18.) Racing on a Saturday arvo in a friendly competition? Taking up design and construction of racing yachts? A sail-making apprenticeship? There is a large industry based around people's enthusiasm for sailing, so you can develop your interest into a career, or you can continue treating it as a very pleasant relaxation/challenge.

It is also possible to get invited to crew on someone's boat — basically as unpaid labour, but in return you get the thrill of sailing anywhere from up and down the coast, or to places like New Zealand or Lord Howe Island.

CIRCUS SKILLS

The WOW factor

For the extrovert performers among you, the answer is obvious … people will look at you and THEY'LL go 'wow'!

For the rest of us, it can be a fun way of gaining enormous confidence in our own abilities, finding out exactly what amazing things our bodies can do, and breaking through the barriers of 'I can't do that'.

Remember, you don't have to perform — you can just acquire the skills.

What does it involve?

Circus performers have an enormous range of skills — from magic acts to whipping cigars out of people's mouths, or shooting people out of cannons (do NOT try the last two). But the 'basic' circus skills are mostly acrobatics, juggling, tightrope walking, and clowning.

How do you go about it?

There are short holiday courses run by the YMCA or the Department of Sport and Recreation (or whatever your state government calls its equivalent). These are run pretty much as demand dictates, so if they aren't on offer these holidays, ring up and suggest that you can find enough people to enrol for a course to make it worth their while. Tumbling, juggling, some low-wire work and clowning would be typical areas that these courses concentrate on.

If you are bitten by the circus bug, then there are some wonderful opportunities for further development, and a quick phone call to the Flying Fruitfly Circus on (02) 9021 7044 (who are based in Albury) is in order. Even if it's impossible to get along to see them, they will know what opportunities are available in different areas (both geographical and skill-based).

What will it cost?

This varies so widely that it is almost pointless to write any down. The private tuition centres tend to cost more than the community-based organisations, but for a short course, $60 will buy you an introduction to circus skills.

Danger level

As with gymnastics and other such sports, injuries — either mild or severe — are possible.

Where can you go from here?

Circus skills are a hot item — there are several tertiary institutions with circus courses, or units devoted to circus skills incorporated into Drama, Theatre or Performing Arts courses. Some, like Swinburne in Melbourne, require you to have a background in competitive gymnastics or classical ballet. Others aren't so specific. There is even a Women's Circus — dedicated to giving women the confidence that comes from testing your boundaries and limitations!

Depending on what you want, you can treat circus skills as a career; a source of weekend money-making doing kid's birthday parties, or corporate launches (juggling and magic acts are a great way to entertain a bored business crowd); or as a hobby that has wonderful spin-offs in terms of fitness, confidence and pleasure. If you are really seriously interested in joining the circus ring Michael Finch of Circus Oz on (03) 9646 8899 to find out more.

HORSE RIDING

The WOW factor

Well, horses of course, and the physical challenge of getting an animal so much larger and more powerful than you are to work with you. For some people it's also where horses can take you.

Who would be interested?

Anyone who loves horses, but also people who like to get out into the bush for a mild adventure, or for those who seek real physical and psychological challenges.

How do you go about it?

A good starting place is a few lessons. If you are considering getting your own horse, it's worth waiting until you're both a competent rider and know a fair bit about horse care. Horses take a heck of a lot of money, and even more time, to look after them properly and you really can't be half-hearted about it. Wait till you are absolutely sure you will still be interested in a few years time.

Look under 'Horses' and 'Horse Riding' in your local phone book for instructors and trail rides. The people you meet there will, of course, be horse mad just like you, and will be able to give you pony club or trail ride contacts.

Another good place to ask is anywhere that sells horse riding equipment. Also look for magazines in the newsagents and in your local library. (The library is the best place to start with magazines, then you don't have to fork out any money to read them.)

If you become a card-carrying fanatic (a full-on horse enthusiast who would rather whinny than talk) you will probably consider taking up some form of competitive, horse-based activity. Whether what you chose is dressage, western riding, polocrosse, endurance riding, show jumping, hacking, one or three day eventing, harness or general showing, you can find that your entire life has been gobbled up, your bank balance depleted and your old friends have drifted off in total boredom. However, to balance out that down-side, you are doing challenging activities (some very challenging indeed — try a 4 a.m. start to a 100 kilometre endurance ride in rough and hilly country by the light of a head lantern or remounting after a fall into water in a cross-country phase of a three-day event). You are with a lot of like-minded people who become life-long friends, who stretch you mentally, physically and emotionally. And even if you 'just' ride around in the bush with your equine friend, there is an enormous and uncommunicable pleasure to be had in your relationship with this powerful quadruped.

Age limit

Because so many kids are into riding, there are lots of organisations that cater just for kids — you shouldn't have to drag your parents along. All they will have to do is get you there, pay for it and explain ten thousand times why they can't afford to buy you a horse or how maybe they will think about it next year or the year after ...

What will it cost?

High if you are considering getting your own horse — you will need somewhere to keep it, you will probably have to buy extra food for it even if it's in a paddock, there will be vet bills, not to mention hiring horse floats and a heck of a lot more. And that's before you start to outfit either yourself or your horse!

Like a lot of activities, if you want, you can spend a king's ransom, but then again, if you haunt saddleries and keep an eye on ads and clearing sales you can equip yourself with surprisingly good and cheap(ish) second-hand gear.

If you decide to compete in any of the equestrian disciplines you have to take entry fees into account, as well as the cost of dragging a float around the countryside, and also all the shampoos and rinses, leather dressing, special show bridles and saddle blankets, bandages, riding jacket and so on and so on.

If you just want to learn to ride, you'll be looking at about $25–$35 for an hour and a half lesson (but prices vary a lot — you may find lessons that are much cheaper — or much more expensive). You can also go on trail rides from about $25–$95 a day (prices for trail rides vary enormously depending on where they are, and who is organising them). A week-long trail-riding expedition, including camping each night, might cost about $700.

On the other hand, if you are a member of a pony club, costs for excursions will be much less but to join you need to have a horse of your own, or at least have one you can borrow.

Danger level

Low to high — mostly horse riding is pretty safe, but even fatal accidents can happen — especially if you are among people who behave like idiots, or think that they are in charge of a fur-covered motorbike, rather than a living, breathing, reacting animal.

Where can you go from here?

There are many jobs with horses, including stud groom, veterinary technician and riding instructor. The racing industry is one of the biggest employers in Australia, and there is a constant demand for young people to work as strappers, training jockeys or race jockeys (a lot of positions, though, are poorly paid, those who are in them are usually very content to be spending their days doing what they love most).

PEGASUS
(RIDING FOR THE DISABLED ASSOCIATION)

Pegasus is an organisation made up entirely of volunteers, with branches in all states and territories.

The WOW factor

If you love horses, this is a chance to work with them — and to share your delight with people who otherwise wouldn't get the opportunity to ride.

Who would be interested?

Anyone who loves horses and helping other people ... it's also a great way to have lots of contact with horses if you don't have one of your own. Or if you are disabled you might want to find out about riding.

One of the favourite hobbies of a friend of mine who is blind, is trail riding. If there is some adventurous activity you are fascinated with, don't be put off by what other people might regard as handicaps.

What will it cost?

Some centres require a membership fee of $10.

What does it involve?

Volunteers can help in classes, or by grooming and feeding the horses. If you want to do more than this, you can train for a Coach's Aide Certificate. If you become really involved you can go on to train as a coach yourself, and you will be examined and awarded a certificate through the Riding for the Disabled Association.

How do you go about it?

Contact your local Riding for the Disabled Centre (look it up in your local phone book) or try the NSW Head Office on (02) 9552 2844.

Age limit

Young people can volunteer from the age of 14 years old.

Danger level

Low to medium. Pegasus horses are specially selected because they are quiet and well-behaved, but a horse is a horse, and accidents can happen.

Where can you go from here?

This is good experience if you are interested in a life with horses or in working with the disabled.

BIRD-WATCHING

The WOW factor

Okay, I'll admit that only a few people reading this book will go 'wow' over spotting birds. But it does require skill, patience, as well as a certain deep, quiet ability. It takes knowledge and experience to recognise bird species — and the more you learn about them, the more fascinating it is to watch their world.

Who would be interested?

Anyone who can tune themselves into the natural world and enjoys just observing.

What does it involve?

Of course you can bird-watch in your own backyard — all you need is a good bird book and you can borrow that from the library. (If you get hooked, then ask for a copy of it for your birthday.) But most bird-watching groups go out into areas where there are a lot of birds — like lakes, swamps or forests.

How do you go about it?

Contact your local bird-watching group — look under 'Clubs' and 'Societies' in the *Yellow Pages*. (Try looking up both bird-watching or ornithology, which is a technical word for bird watching, or even natural history.) You might also contact your local (or nearest) environment centre — they often have a list of clubs and societies involved with birds, animals or the bush. (There isn't much point my listing any bird-watching groups here, as the contact address and phone number for most of them is that of their president or secretary — and these can change from year to year.)

The Bird Observers Club of Australia has branches in many parts of Australia. You can contact them at P.O. Box 185, Nunawading, Victoria 3131, or phone them on (03) 9877 5342. Membership costs $48 a year, but concessions are available. They run bird-watching outings for beginners on Saturdays but you would need to coax a friendly adult to take you.

If you are really interested in birds (or birds, insects and animals) you might also consider joining the Gould League.

The Gould League is a great place to learn about birds, animals, insects, and the environment. They publish a wide range of books and posters for kids about birds, plants and animals, and they send out newsletters. There are branches of the Gould League in South Australia, Western Australia, Queensland, Victoria and New South Wales. They don't organise expeditions, but you will get a lot of information in the newsletters.

If you want to join the Gould League, write to them at: Gould League, Genoa Street, Moorabbin, Victoria 3189, or phone (03) 9532 0909 or send a fax to (03) 9532 2860.

Membership costs $9.95 and you will receive a certificate, *The Backyard Wildlife Book*, mini-binoculars, a magpie badge, two newsletters, and discounts on Gould League books. (They also have some great stuff on building nesting boxes for birds or possums — just thought I'd put that in as I've used some of their designs!)

Age limit

While bird-watching groups usually have junior membership, which costs less than adult membership, they usually don't cater especially for kids. This means that if you want to go on a bird hunt, you will need to convince an adult to take you, at least the first time. Although, if you are extraordinarily enthusiastic, you may find an adult bird-watcher who would be willing to take you under their wing (joke intended) and transport you to other bird-watching events — but this will have to be done in negotiation with your parents and guardians. Just remember that, as with everything, if you are enthusiastic about something, other enthusiasts will love to help you.

What will it cost?

Low. Basically you will need a bird identification book and transport — although a good pair of binoculars would be a nice thing to get for Christmas.

Danger level

Low.

Where can you go from here?

If you are really into bird-watching, you might want to consider studying zoology at university when you finish school, or becoming a National Parks ranger.

R.S.P.C.A. AUSTRALIA

The WOW factor

You will be helping to care for animals that have been lost or abused, learning about animal care, and working with other people who feel like you do.

Who would be interested?

People who love animals, can cope with the messy work and with the sad fact that some animals may have to be put down.

What does it involve?

Anything from cleaning cages to office work — depending on what's needed.

How do you go about it?

There are branches in every state and territory, so a call to your local branch (look up the R.S.P.C.A. in the phone book) will give you more details. The Head Office telephone number is (02) 6282 8300 and the fax number is (02) 6282 8311. Or have a look at their website at: http://www.rspca.org.au — it has links to the R.S.P.C.A offices in each state.

Age limit

This varies from state to state. In the ACT junior members are under 16 years old, and can join for $10 a year. Members who are over 10 years old can be rostered on to help at the animal shelter. Excursions are organised for junior members.

In NSW juniors are under 12 years old and can join for $3 a year. Youth support runs from 12–18 years of age and costs $5 a year. Volunteers must be over 13 years old.

Danger level

Low.

Where can you go from here?

It's good experience if you're interested in a career involving animals — whether as a professional animal welfare worker with the R.S.P.C.A., as a National Parks and Wildlife officer, or as a vet or veterinary technician.

APOLOGY

This book is just a taste of the things that kids can get involved in (i.e. they are the ones that occurred to me and any passing friends and relatives while I was writing the book).

I know that there will be a heck of a lot of stuff that I haven't thought of but if you know of anything, please do let me know (care of the publisher's address in the front of this book). If I can, I will put it in the next edition.

ANIMAL WELFARE LEAGUE

This section is also for all similar animal welfare organisations in all capital cities and most regional centres.

The WOW factor

A lot of the work will be messy, tedious and repetitive but you will know that you are doing good work and each day will have the small joys that working with animals can offer.

Who would be interested?

If you have an affinity with animals, you would possibly enjoy working with them and learning about animal care.

What does it involve?

The NSW Animal Welfare League — which can be contacted at (02) 9606 9333 — operates an animal care centre at West Hoxton. They use volunteers over the age of 16 to help with walking the dogs, grooming both the dogs and the cats, as well as general feeding and cleaning chores. If you have an adult who is willing to accompany you, then you can begin to help at a younger age. They also take students through school-based, work experience programs.

How do you go about it?

Look up 'Animal Welfare Organisations' in the *Yellow Pages* of your local phone book.

What will it cost?

This will vary with each organisation but is usually low to negligible.

Danger level

Low — as long as you don't mind the odd scratch or bite from frightened animals.

Where can you go from here?

It's good experience if you are interested in a career involving animals, whether as a professional animal welfare worker with the R.S.P.C.A., a National Parks and Wildlife officer, or as a vet or veterinary technician.

CARING FOR NATIVE ANIMALS

The WOW factor

It's an incredible privilege to spend time with a wild animal — a chance that most people never get. You may meet sugar gliders, wombats, kangaroos, magpies, lizards, snakes, frogs ...

Who would be interested?

Anyone who loves animals — and who has the self-discipline to look after them properly, and the strength to accept that, all too often, injured or orphaned animals die.

What does it involve?

Members of WIRES, Wildcare and similar associations look after native animals and birds that have been injured or orphaned. These include animals such as baby wombats that have been found still living in their mothers' pouches after the mother has been killed on the road or attacked by dogs.

Members of these organisations also do all sorts of rescues, including; saving injured lizards trapped in drainpipes; rescuing joeys and bats; freeing cockatoos strung up in trees; and even fishing snakes out of water tanks.

The animals that come into their care are not kept as pets. When ready, they are released gradually so that they can get used to being back in the wild.

Caring for an orphaned baby animal isn't easy — you need a lot of training and an enormous amount of time and dedication to keep them clean, to feed them every two hours or so — including at night — and give them the care and cuddling they need.

How do you go about it?

There are many organisations in each state involved in caring for wildlife. These include WIRES — you can look up WIRES in your local phone book to see if there is a branch near you, or check their website (it has loads of great information and a list of all offices) at: http://www.wires.webcentral.com.au. The ACT Wildlife Foundation can be contacted by phone on: (02) 6296 3114 and write to Fauna Rescue of SA at: P.O. Box 241, Modbury North, South Australia 5092. Fauna Rescue also have a FANTASTIC website, which is jam-packed full of information. You can find it at: http://members.iweb.net.au/~ross/.

Wildcare, in Queanbeyan, NSW (for the rescue, rehabilitation and release of native animals into the wild) runs a children's club called Wallabats for primary-aged children. They provide a very cheery and informative bimonthly newsletter (full of animals, birds and flowers to be looked for at that time of the year, hints for identification, activities, book reviews, etc.), and a badge. They will also send members of Wildcare into the classroom to introduce kids to local wildlife and their environment. Contact Margie Burke, (02) 6299 1966, or Queanbeyan Wildcare Inc., P.O. Box 1404, Queanbeyan, NSW 2620. Wildcare has a website: http://www.effect.net.au/wildcare and a special kids' webpage: http://www.npac.syr.edu/textbook/kidsweb.

If you can't find anything about caring for wildlife in the phone book, call your local police station — they often have a number that people can ring if they find injured wildlife on the road. Or contact your local vet and ask them who they contact locally for injured wildlife.

Age limit

You have to be over 18 to be given responsibility for an injured animal — but if you show that you are caring, willing and hard working, I'm sure many adults would be incredibly glad of your help!

What will it cost?

Younger people can join Friends of WIRES for $30 a year, and you receive newsletters, a magnet and a badge. Wildcare costs $120 a year for adults, but only $10 if you want to be a member of Wallabats (remember that these costs may have changed by the time you enquire about it).

If you can't afford any money at all, and you still badly want to help, it's still worthwhile contacting the organisations and offering your services.

Danger level

Low — though, again, you might get the odd bite or scratch. (Wombats, for example can give you a nip, just to say 'hello'.) And be aware that it can be incredibly distressing when a baby animal you have been caring for suddenly dies — I know, because it's happened to me several times.

Where can you go from here?

These associations will teach you an enormous amount about the wild animals you may be caring for — which is useful if you intend to go into any career with animals, or become a National Parks Ranger.

A PASSION FOR PLATYPUS

I first got to know my husband on a platypus hunt, so I'm biased — but if you're fascinated by the platypus and want to know more, or you simply want to spot them in the wild, you might consider joining Friends of the Platypus.

The WOW factor

A fascinating creature (if you are into platypuses) that most people know almost nothing about — much less ever having seen one.

What does it involve?

Friends of the Platypus produce a newsletter containing news of platypus sightings and research. You also get a book when you join that will tell you more than you ever dreamed you would know about platypuses. There are also platypus-spotting outings — but these seem to be limited to Victoria.

How do you go about it?

Contact Friends of the Platypus, c/o- Australian Platypus Conservancy, P.O. Box 84, Whittlesea Victoria 3757, or phone them on (03) 9716 1626. (Of course, you may also come across a platypus while you are bushwalking or camping.)

What will it cost?

To join Friends of the Platypus, it costs $30 for an adult, $45 for a family, and $20 for a full-time student.

Age limit

You need to be over 8 to go platypus spotting — and you will also need to coax a helpful adult along. You need to be able to sit still and watch for long periods ... but on the other hand to see these creatures play, hunt, or even just doze can be absolutely thrilling — if, like me, you happen to be that way inclined.

Where can you go from here?

You can pursue a career in zoology, vet science or technology, or zoo keeping. You might think about becoming a National Parks ranger, or working in soil conservation to preserve or rehabilitate our waterways.

MUSHING

Otherwise known as dogsled racing.

The WOW factor

It can be completely exhilarating when you scoot along at what feels like very high speeds indeed, through pine forests with a happy dog (or dogs), and you feel that particular thrill that some of us feel when communicating and cooperating with other species.

What does it involve?

Mushing began as dogsleds on snow, but has now been popularised in other countries and climates (i.e. ones that are a heck of a lot hotter) with racing dogs (usually malamutes or huskies but not exclusively so) on dirt tracks. The dogs are harnessed to a light scooter, with a handler running and riding along.

The dogs begin mushing over short distances (e.g. 500 metres), but as they, and you, become fit they tackle distances of about four kilometres.

One very important thing to remember is that mushing is always a team sport, and the driver must scoot on the flat, run up the hills, and not allow the scooter to run into the dog on the downhill slope. It is most important that both dog and driver enjoy the sport and that neither is pushed beyond their limits!

How do you get involved?

You need a scooter, a dog (of a reasonable size, age and build), a properly adjusted harness, and a bunjee to attach the dog to the scooter. You also need a helmet and parental permission, and you must be at least 12 years old. And preferably choose a day when the temperature is not going to rise above 15°C.

The Canine Council or Kennel Club in your state will be able to put you in touch with the organisers of your nearest mushing group. In our area there are the

Canberra Sled Dog Club, the Siberian Husky Club of NSW and the Alaskan Malamute Club of NSW — all of whom organise races on State forest tracks.

How much will it cost?

It would be a good idea to have a taste of this sport before investing a lot of money in the gear.

This means making yourself known to those already mushing, making yourself useful at meets and helping with training and get-fit programmes. In many instances, training the dogs requires two people (one on the scooter and the other on a bike), and you could offer to be the second person.

Where can you go from here?

Well, nowhere really (although there is at least one commercial operation giving dogsled rides up above the snowline) but you can have a great time, feel fit, and enjoy your dog in a different setting.

If you feel like a dogsled ride in the snow, there is a commercial dogsled ride at Fall's Creek in Victoria. It costs $120 for two adults plus a smallish kid for a 10km run pulled by eight Alaskan malamutes. Phone (03) 5754 4880 for more information. (I used to dream of a cart pulled by giant dogs to take me to school when I was very small.)

DOG SHOWING

The WOW factor

Obviously, if you are fiercely competitive, then winning will give you a buzz. But dog showing and, more particularly, the Junior Dog Handling classes, will teach you to perform in public, win with grace, lose with dignity, and take responsibility for yourself and an animal.

What does it involve?

No, you don't need a dog! (And no, I don't mean getting your best friend to dress up as one either!)

If you want to compete in most sections of dog shows, you do need a dog of your own … this usually means your parents must be breeding pedigreed dogs. But to enter Junior Dog Handling classes you only have to win the trust of someone who will lend you a dog with which to compete.

Junior Dog Handling is sponsored very generously by Pedigree Pal in Australia and is open to kids between the ages of 7 and 18. There is no charge to enter, and you enter on the day of the show. It is now organised nationally by the National Junior Dog Handlers Club, and the National Coordinator is Judy Chapman who can be contacted on (08) 8338 2512.

Anyone can enter a class at any qualifying show — country kids can check out where their nearest qualifying show is and head for that, and city kids will have a wide range of shows to choose from. Those who win at a qualifying show can then compete at the State Finals. From there the successful competitors proceed to the National Finals (which are usually held between September and October) and the winner is then eligible to go on to compete at Crufts in Birmingham, in the UK, in March.

There are very few opportunities for children to compete for prizes as glamorous and generous as this — a trip for two to England, with opportunities for sightseeing, as well as competing against other kids from up to 30 countries.

Depending on the breed of dog you are showing, you will lead the dog into the ring showing it off to its best advantage. Small dogs are put on a table for the judge's inspection, and larger breeds are inspected on the ground — they must look alert and eager, but be at all times under control and biddable. There are classes in dog handling organised for junior handlers in some states, but in others you might have to join the adult classes. Phone your state Canine Council or Kennel Club for details.

What will it cost?

From nothing to a fortune. The entry to any Pedigree Pal Junior Dog Handling event is free. Pedigreed dogs who are show-ring winners are worth real money, but fortunately you can become involved with Junior Dog Handling without owning a dog — although most people do own a dog, or soon become owners. The generosity of dog people is legendary, and if you are trustworthy and keen, you will be allowed access to dogs to show.

Where can you go from here?

The world of pedigreed dogs has many opportunities for those who are devoted — training, showing, breeding, and, of course, judging. Some people make a living from it; the rest are devoted owners who derive enormous pleasure, and sometimes a little money, from their hobby.

MARINE ANIMALS AND THE SEA

If you love the sea and want to know more about it, as well as play in it, try looking it up at: http://www.mesa.edu.au or http://www.geocities.com/EnchantedForest/dell/8662/rockyshore.html.

These are excellent websites and will give you lots of information, as well as other places you might contact. You could also contact The Marine Education Society of Australasia, at P.O. Box 461, East Bentleigh, Vic 3165 or phone them on (03) 9503 9823, although this is really more for teachers than kids.

LOOKING AFTER
THE ENVIRONMENT

ENVIRONMENT CENTRES

Environment centres are a resource for groups interested in conservation and looking after the environment. They are also for bushwalking, bicycling, and other groups who enjoy the environment as well. They provide libraries, meeting places, magazines; they undertake research ... and a lot of other things.

The WOW factor

You are helping to look after the environment.

Who would be interested?

Anyone with a real feeling of commitment for environmental health and change.

What does it involve?

Environment centres always need help, as they are mostly run and financed by volunteers. You might help in the library, or man the bookshop, or sell stuff at street stalls, or help with research, or just stuff newsletters into envelopes for an hour or two.

How do you go about it?

Find the number for your local environment centre by looking up 'Environmental Groups' in the *Yellow Pages*, or 'Organisations' (try conservation or environmental). Then ring them up, tell them your name, how old you are, and what you're interested in — then ask how you can help.

What will it cost?

Your time.

THE AUSTRALIAN TRUSTS FOR
CONSERVATION

The WOW factor

Helping to look after the environment.

Who would be interested?

Anyone who likes the outdoors and has a social conscience.

What does it involve?

The Australian Trusts for Conservation (1800 032 501) welcomes adolescents and their families into their programmes of tree planting and weed eradication, revegetation, seed collection and so forth. Under 16s must be accompanied by an adult and there is no charge for one-day outings. Participants are picked up at a meeting point and transported to the site — bring your own tucker. Weekend workshops are also organised, for which adults are charged $20 and students up to the age of 15 are charged $10. Some schools (primary and secondary) have their own programmes organised through the Trust. Visit the website http://www.atcv.com.au.

Danger level

Low.

Where can you go from here?

You'll learn a heck of a lot about plant and animal ecology, bush care, and weed eradication — all of which would be very useful for anyone contemplating a career in botany, zoology or environmental science.

CLEAN UP AUSTRALIA

The WOW factor

Turning a rubbish-infested bit of land into something that looks good.

What does it involve?

On Clean Up Australia Day, volunteers all over Australia meet and collect rubbish from their target area — not just from parks and along roads, but also dragging car bodies and supermarket trolleys out of lakes and creeks.

How do you go about it?

Ring your council for details — and if they aren't involved hassle them until they buckle at the knees. Clean Up Australia Day is also supported by Westpac, so you can contact your local Westpac bank too. Often schools are involved in Clean up Australia, so ask at yours.

OTHER ENVIRONMENT GROUPS

There are many other environment groups such as Greening Australia (contact the CSIRO for local details), local Landcare groups, Streamwatch, and Beachwatch. All are contactable through your state's equivalent of the Department of Water and Land Management and Conservation.

All these groups welcome young people, and you can be actively involved in water testing, tree planting, weed eradication, etc.

The best way to join these programmes is to get your school involved — if you can find a teacher to coordinate it all. These activities can become part of your lesson time.

The Threatened Species Network collects data on vulnerable species of animals, insects and plants. It then organises to apply pressure to politicians and planners who will affect any species that might already be under enormous pressure. It has branches in all states and some branches accept volunteers, including children. The sort of activities you would be doing may include a limited amount of hands-on animal work, but most of the work would probably be office based — answering the telephone, researching, sorting and filing, helping with newsletters, and updating the website. Here are the current state contact numbers; Tasmania — (03) 6234 3552; Victoria — (03) 9650 8296; NSW/ACT — (02) 9281 5515; Queensland — (07) 3221 0573; SA — (08) 8223 5155; NT — (08) 8952 1541; and WA — (08) 9387 6444.

Their website can be found at http://nccnsw.org.au/member/tsn/ and is well worth visiting.

See also Northern Territory Junior Rangers and Junior Police Rangers on page 186 and The Duke of Edinburgh Award on page 183.

SCIENTIFIC CHALLENGES

THE DOUBLE HELIX CLUB

The Double Helix Club is run by CSIRO and it is very hard to describe how great it is in just a few paragraphs.

The WOW factor

All sorts of them — from making backyard rockets, to being part of Australia-wide experiments, to just learning the how and why ...

Who would be interested?

Anyone interested in science — and by science I mean research about anything from animals, to asteroids, volcanoes, vampire bats, or the second law of thermodynamics. (If you know what that is you'd love The Double Helix club. If you don't then you *need* the club!)

What does it involve?

When you are a member of The Double Helix club you:

- Get the *Double Helix* — a 40 page, full-colour science magazine that comes out six times a year. And it is definitely not a sort of 'come on kiddies let's learn about amoebas' affair. It is really GOOD — you get fascinating stories about modern scientific discoveries (the sort of stuff you won't see on TV or read in papers); career profiles of scientists — not just the white coat in a lab-type ones, but marine researchers, or museum curators, or people stuck down in the Antarctic; there are good competitions; and activities and projects which can range from ones that are good for a giggle, to making your own radio receiver for less than $10.

- Get to go on 'Double Helix Events' — excursions, activity days and other science experiences in capital cities and regional centres all over Australia. There are over 250 events in capital cities alone including: using scanning electron microscopes, trying out a flight simulator, and presentations by microsurgeons, astronauts and some of Australia's top scientists from very different fields.

- Get hands-on sessions at CSIRO Science Education Centres in capital cities.
- Get to take part in national experiments. In 1993, for example, the Earthworms Down Under experiment provided data that would have taken over a decade to collect, if over 2000 kids hadn't done most of the work. Earthworms Down Under resulted in Australia's first earthworm key — so now farmers know what type of earthworms are where, and how to encourage them. (Earthworms are extremely important in sustainable farming.)

Other experiments include the Termite Tally (termites happily munch their way through houses and other dead wood — and you really need to know what sort of termite occurs where before you can work out how to stop them from making your house their lunch); Dung Beetle Crusade (dung beetles break up dung, which stops flies from laying their eggs in it); mapping the distribution of fruit flies (which lay those interesting little 'worms' in fruit); the release and monitoring of a weevil that will help control water hyacinth (an incredible weed that's taking over many of our waterways); and saving the Richmond Birdwing Butterfly.

Double Helix has also been featured on the top rating TV show *Totally Wild* and on *Hey, Hey it's Saturday*.

How do you go about it?

Contact the CSIRO's Double Helix Science Club, by writing to them at: P.O. Box 225, Dickson ACT 2602, phoning them on (02) 6276 6643, sending them a fax at (02)6276 6641, or an e-mail to education_programs@helix.csiro.au or check out the website at: http://www.csiro.au/helix. It's got all the latest club news, heaps of experiments and hot science sites to surf.

Age limit

Double Helix is really for kids over 10 (although if you're under 10 and really interested, don't let that stop you).

What will it cost?

It costs $25 a year (although brothers and sisters get a discounted $20 each) to join. If you can't afford it, pester your school library or local library to subscribe so you can read the *Double Helix* and find out when the activities are on.

Danger level

Low ... the experiments have been very carefully selected to reduce the danger of you blowing up the house.

Where can you go from here?

If you are interested in any scientific field at all — from astronomy to geology, medicine, zoology, botany and also a heck of a lot of scientific fields and jobs you probably don't even know exist — you will get a good head start with Double Helix.

P.S. CSIRO also puts out *Scientriffic* magazine. It's for kids aged about 7–11, and for families to read and enjoy together. It's also great — it will tell you about the fascinating world you live in, including dinosaurs, space science and our environment. It will give you amazing and easy experiments to try at home, and great competitions with decent prizes.

Scientriffic costs $19.95 a year. Check it out at: http://www.csiro.au/scientriffic or write to CSIRO, P.O. Box 225, Dickson ACT 2602, or phone them on (02) 6276 6643 or send a fax to (02) 6276 6641. (Cheques should be made out to CSIRO Education.)

HUNTING FOR DINOSAURS
(THE DINOSAUR CLUB)

The WOW factor

You can't get much more wow! than dinosaurs. (Did you know that in the last three years, the three largest meat eating dinosaurs that ever lived were discovered?)

What does it involve?

Okay, you can't exactly hunt live dinosaurs anymore, but you can find traces, including fossils and fossil footprints of ancient dinosaurs and even older creatures. The challenge here isn't to avoid being eaten by one — it's to find their remains, work out what they looked like, what they ate, how they bred . . .

How do you go about it?

Join The Dinosaur Club. You will get two magazines a year and some branches put out regular newsletters as well. The magazines will tell you about all the latest in dinosaur research, often the sort of stuff you'll never find in newspapers or magazines, and often, not even in books.

You'll also get an information kit which has information and activity material, plus the latest copy of the magazine. (Past copies can be bought for $2.20.)

Members are also invited to talks, workshops, new displays at museums, and may also get the opportunity to go on 'digs' — in other words, you get to actually help look for dinosaur fossils. This isn't available at all branches, though — it just depends on what dinosaur hunting activity is going on in your area. (If you're keen enough, though, you might be able to join in another branch's activities.)

By the way, The Dinosaur Club is for adults as well as kids (membership costs the same), so you definitely won't find that it is a 'just for kids' affair with lots of 'let's colour in the dinosaurs' — this is real stuff, for people of any age who are fascinated by that aspect of our past.

The Dinosaur Club's nerve centre is in the care of the Western Australian Museum, Francis Street, Perth, WA 6000 (phone 08 - 9328 4411). South Australians should contact that address too. The other branches are:

New South Wales: c/o- Margery Phair, Australian Museum Dinosaur Club, 6 College St, Sydney, NSW 2000 (phone 02 - 9320 6000).

Tasmania: The Dinosaur Club, c/o- Alisanne Ramsden, Queen Victoria Museum and Art Gallery, Wellington St, Launceston, Tasmania 7250 (phone 03 - 6331 6777).

ACT: The Dinosaur Club, c/o- Jeff Death, National Dinosaur Museum, Barton Highway, Gungahlin ACT 2912 (phone 02 - 6230 2655).

Victoria: The Dinosaur Club, c/o- Dr Vickers-Rich, Monash Science Centre, Monash University, Clayton, Vic 3168 (phone 03 - 9905 1370).

QLD/NT: The Dinosaur Club, Queensland Museum Association Inc, PO Box 3300, South Brisbane, QLD 4101 (phone 07 - 3840 7635).

What will it cost?

For individual membership it is $12 a year, although group membership (if your class or club wants to join) is $20 a year.

Danger level

Low, due to the extremely dead state of dinosaurs.

Where can you go from here?

If you are really keen on dinosaurs, you might consider a career in palaeontology, or becoming a curator in a museum.

SEARCHING FOR ALIENS (SETI)

The WOW factor

Okay, are they out there, or aren't they? And if aliens do exist, are they like humans? Does intelligent life HAVE to be like humans? Are they trying to contact us too? And what would it be like to be the first person on Earth to find out?

Who would be interested?

Anyone who is into computers or aliens ...

What does it involve?

Using your computer to help search for radio signals from another planet. Yes, I know that it sounds like something from a sci-fi book or movie or the X-Files, but this is real!

How do you go about it?

SETI@home is a scientific experiment that harnesses the power of hundreds of thousands of Internet-connected computers in the Search for Extraterrestrial Intelligence (SETI). You can participate by running a program that downloads and analyses radio-telescope data.

There is a small, but captivating, chance that your computer will detect the faint murmur of a civilization beyond Earth. If you want to be the one to find out that we are not alone in the universe, then SETI@home is the challenge for you.

SETI (Search for Extra Terrestrial Intelligence) Australia Centre can be contacted at: http://www.seti.uws.edu.au or you can telephone (02) 4620 3488 or fax (02) 4628 1493. You can even write to them. Send a letter to:

Carol Oliver, Executive Officer,
SETI Australia,
UWS Macarthur,
P.O. Box 555,
Campbelltown
NSW 2560.

If you want to enquire about using your computer for some SETI research, then send an e-mail to: c.oliver@uws.edu.au

The SETI Research & Community Development Institute is based in Brisbane, Queensland and can be contacted via the website at: http://www.seti.org.au. This is worth a look (groovy home page), but it is a privately financed research organisation, and it is really aimed at engineers, technicians, and computer programmers, rather than kids.

What will it cost?

You will have to have reasonable computing power to be able to help.

Danger level

Low (assuming the aliens are not on our doorstep).

Where can you go from here?

At the very least you will learn valuable computer skills, plus a heck of a lot about radio signals and the universe. And at the other end of the scale, well, it's a big universe out there — who knows where you will end up …

ALTERNATIVE TECHNOLOGY

The WOW factor

You are not just learning how to do something — but also how to do it in the most sustainable, and often imaginative, manner!

Who would be interested?

Anyone who likes tinkering with mechanical things or is interested in helping the world find technologies we can safely use for the next few centuries. Also, people who want to know how to build their own homes and power systems, without having to borrow money from the bank and spend the rest of their lives paying it back.

What does it involve?

Alternative or 'appropriate' technology is about doing things in the best way — which isn't necessarily the way that most people do it.

Many people — like me — believe that the way we get our power now is wasteful and polluting; that the way we build houses now is expensive and boring; that it's a waste of good fertiliser when we send it out to sea to pollute the ocean and our beaches, — it could be used to feed us or forests instead. I could go on and on for pages!

I live in a house that we mostly made ourselves; we get our power from solar panels, but also from a home-made water wheel. We do things like this partly because we feel it's best for the environment, but also because it's fun and fascinating — and it's really rewarding to feel that you are in charge of such essential aspects of your own life as your house, your power, even your water and sewerage.

How do you go about it?

High schools sometimes give courses in alternative technology or solar power … if yours doesn't and you are interested, it is worth, at least, making your interest known. Maybe it would be possible to have such a course at your school — or guest lecturers to talk to you about it. You may also prefer to switch to another school which does have courses like these. (But think very hard about that, because there are other points to consider too, like friends, and how far away it is, and what other subjects you will be doing. There are other ways of getting involved in alternative technology — just keep reading.)

There are also many alternative technology races, challenges, and competitions — from solar boat and car construction and races, to building solar gliders, to recycled organics conferences, and renewable energy fairs. Plus there are all sorts of evening and weekend courses in everything from non-toxic paints, to how to make your own solar hot water system or mudbrick house.

The best way to find out about these is to look up the Australian Alternative Technology Association website: http://www.netspace.net.au/~altec.

If you find a race or challenge that catches your fancy, you might be able to convince a teacher, parent or Scout group to enter one of them. Gather together a group of interested and willing workers, ask local businesses to donate advice or materials, and off you go! Every solar boat race, car race, etc., I've been to has been lots of fun ... and even when you are marooned in the middle of a lake when your boat conks out, it's fun and challenging to work out why and how it happened — and to improve your design.

This is one area where amateurs can really contribute to changing technology — in an area where inspiration is desperately needed!

You might also like to either subscribe to the Australian Alternative Technology Association magazine, *Renew*, or look it up in the local library, and if it is not there, ask your school library to subscribe to it.

Although it's aimed at adults, there is lots in it that technically minded kids will enjoy — our copy is always snaffled by several of the kids who visit our house regularly.

The issue I have in front of me includes stuff about:

- A young woman who built her own home — toilet, power system, hot water and all for under $10 000 (which means if you and a friend live on the smell of an oily rag for a year, and both have jobs, you can easily save enough to build your own home without borrowing, which was how I built mine. Of course, you do have to have land to build it on ... another two years of saving! But after that — no mortgage!)
- How to make your own fuel from vegetable oil, plus a vegetable-oil-powered tractor.
- A report on the great electric bicycle rally — it sounded like incredible fun.
- How to make your own grey water recycling system — in other words, use 'used' water in your house to water the garden without spreading all sorts of yuk and diseases.
- Noel's Treasures from trash, which is in every issue ... how to make something weird or useful out of rubbish.
- An article on 'How to make your own Stirling engine.' Most engines are internal combustion engines, they burn fuel inside combustion chambers. A Stirling engine is an external combustion engine, and you can make it from what's basically a heap of junk ... and if you have managed to follow this explanation so far, the chances are you'll enjoy doing it. Then there is hooking the engine up to run who knows what ... I am NOT mechanically minded (although that hasn't stopped me running my house on solar power, or building stone walls).

Renew costs $5.50 an issue, and it's one of my favourite magazines. The address to write to is P.O. Box 2001,

Lygon St, North Brunswick East, Victoria 3057 (but don't worry — there's stuff in it for all over Australia) or you can phone (03) 9388 9311 or e-mail altec@netspace.net.au

If you are really into alternative energy, building, and growing stuff, you might also like to have a look at the *Owner Builder* magazine, *Earthgarden* (I write a column for it) and *Grassroots*. You will find them all in the newsagents, and also probably in your local library — if you can't find them on the shelves, ask the librarian if the library subscribes to them. If they don't, flick through them at the newsagents to see if it's worth asking your parents to buy them in order to contribute to your general education and well-being. (Newsagents hate it when people do this — they say that they are not a library! If people are interested then they should buy the magazine! But often flicking through a whole range of magazines on the shelf is a great way to find things you might be interested in, from chook breeding to weightlifting. And if you do find a magazine you like you will then become a regular customer!)

Age limit

Nope ... just about everything is open to everyone — and even in races that are open to major companies from all around the world, kid's entries often do suprisingly well!

What will it cost?

It can be high for raw materials, but often it's not — many of the materials can be scavenged or recycled. (That's part of what it's about.)

For more major endeavours, local businesses and groups like the Lions or Rotary Clubs may sponsor you — that is, help pay for all, or some, of the materials, and even travel costs if necessary. But it may just be that some of your effort will also have to go into making money.

Where can you go from here?

If you shine in one of the challenges, you might just come to the notice of someone who will offer you a job ... but even without this, there are now an enormous number of job opportunities in alternative technology — everything from installing alternative power systems, or manufacturing and designing composting toilets, to designing electric cars for major companies, to building mudbrick houses. You can also open an alternative technology supply shop, research more effective solar panels or wind generators — or cheaper ways of making them and a lot more besides.

If you are interested in anything from electronics to engineering, including architecture, chemistry, physics, agriculture, building and probably a heck of a lot more, there is a niche for you in alternative technology.

CHALLENGES WITH COMPUTERS

I could write a whole book on challenges with computers ... and I'm not even particularly, a computer-type person! But just in case you don't already know a lot more about computers than I do, here are just a few of the challenges with your computer you can do. You can:

- Join a specialist chat group that talks about anything from astrophysics to model aeroplanes, or a chat group that just chats.
- You can publish your own book, stories or poetry on the web.
- You can set up webpages for your school, local council, or any worthwhile group that you are involved in. (I know two kids who have a small business setting up webpages. They earn quite a nice amount of money each holidays — but then, they are very, very good at it!)
- Find out more about just about any subject that interests you, from the chance of a meteor crashing on the earth, to the website of your favourite author, to what might be the secret recipe for Coca-Cola.
- You can use specialist programmes to design your own birthday cards, or learn to fly a plane or dive a submarine, or write your own music.
- You can have a penfriend on the other side of the world, and 'talk' to each other each weekend.
- You can design your own exciting computer games (and if that works, you may make a lot of money).
- You can search out holiday sites, costs and ways of getting there, and organise your family's next holiday.
- You can also find some really snazzy sites: like hunting for the Loch Ness monster by watching live images from the loch (http://www.lochness.co.uk/livecam/index.html). There is also a camera at the Mount St Helen's volcano — you might catch its

next eruption on: http://www.fs.us/gpnf.mshnum.
volcanocam/volcanocam2.htm.

- Look for live lions and rhinos at: http://www.africa
  cam.co.za or music at: http://www.imusic.com or
  dogs at: http://www.pcug.org.au/~shaker/dogs.htm or
  http://www.wwwins.net.au/dogsdownunder.html or ...
  well, I could go on forever!

How do you go about it?

If you don't have a computer at home, most local
libraries have computers with Internet access. You
usually have to pay a small fee to use them, but your
library will also show you how to use the computer, and
possibly even how to register your own e-mail address
(hotmail ones — http://www.hotmail.com — are free).

Ask your teachers if there is any way you can have
supervised access to the school computers for an hour
after school, before school, or for the odd morning
during school holidays.

HELPING OTHERS

HELPING SOCIAL WELFARE
ORGANISATIONS

The WOW factor

There is a 'wow' in helping others — you get to feel incredibly good about yourself.

What does it involve?

First, find a charity you would like to support. (I usually choose a different charity each year and make one large donation.)

What do you feel most deeply about? Who would you like to help most? Kids with cancer, injured animals, refugees, villages overseas that don't have good water supplies ... there are many, many different areas where help is needed. Choose the one that really strikes into your heart, then contact the head office and ask them how you can help.

Most things available for kids involve fundraising activities — doorknocking, street stalls, etc. St Vincent de Paul also encourages kids to do things like donating home-made cards or presents.

Two good places to start are at your local school or church — just say that you are interested in helping others and ask if there are any local projects they know about that you could help with?

You could also look up contact numbers in the *Yellow Pages* of the phone book under 'Organisations — Disadvantaged Groups Aid' or 'Organisations — Family Welfare'. Some of the organisations listed will be government agencies which don't accept volunteer help, so be prepared to ring a few. Also, do tell your parents, or some intelligent adult, what you are doing, just in case you get involved with someone weird.

How do you go about it?

Three wonderful organisations are Amnesty International, World Vision and St Vincent de Paul.

Amnesty International works for the human rights of people throughout the world, including people who are imprisoned because of their beliefs, colour, sex, ethnic origin, language, or religion. Kids can volunteer their time, help raise money, or even form their own school branch. Call 1800 028 357 or look up their website at: http://www.amnesty.org.au.

World Vision helps you to sponsor a child, and their family and community, in Africa, Asia and Latin America. You could either sponsor a child yourself, or you and your friends might like to do it together. You could also organise your class or school to sponsor a child. Call 13 23 40 for more details — or look up the website at: http://www.worldvision.org.au.

You can form a St Vincent de Paul Youth Group at your school. You can then help with fundraising for St Vincent de Paul's work in the community by running raffles, casual clothes days, cakestalls, coin lines, etc. You can also help with visits to nursing homes, help run picnic days, or attend youth camps as a leader for disadvantaged kids, work at your local St Vincent de Paul Centre, cut lawns for senior citizens, or organise free breakfasts for kids who don't get any.

Contact your local St Vincent de Paul Centre (look it up in the phone book) or e-mail vinyouth@ozemail.com.au to find the centre closest to you and other information about starting a group.

You might also look up the website for the International Committee of the Red Cross at: http://www.icrc.org.

What will it cost?

Your time and caring.

Danger level

Low, physically. Be prepared to have your heart tugged at least a bit.

Where can you go from here?

If you like helping others you might consider studying social work, counselling, psychology, speech therapy, musical therapy or even medicine, nursing or physiotherapy.

HELPING PEOPLE YOURSELF

If you would rather do something yourself — not just collect money — you could also:

- Plant a flower garden at school, so that you can grow flowers for people in hospitals or in nursing homes.
- Form a choir — even if it's just six of you — and sing carols at hospitals and nursing homes.
- Make biscuits or home-made cakes to take to people in hospitals or nursing homes.
- Ring up the Royal Blind Society and offer your services reading to someone who is blind.
- Contact the Guide Dog Association and offer to look after guide dog puppies until they are old enough to be trained, or look after elderly guide dogs that have been 'retired' because they are too old to work any more. (These are lovely dogs who deserve a lot of love and comfort after all their years of helping people.)
- Offer to tutor kids in a subject that you are good at (ask your teacher how you might go about this).
- See also Pegasus on page 82 and WIRES, Wildcare, the R.S.P.C.A. and other animal welfare organisations in chapter two.

JUNIOR BUSH FIRE BRIGADES

The WOW factor

Danger, excitement, the thrill of learning how to face our greatest, most ancient enemy (fire), and the satisfaction of working with a team. Volunteer bush fire fighters are often truly heroic, although most of the time their heroism isn't widely acknowledged.

Who would be interested?

Anyone reasonably fit who lives in a bush fire-prone area.

What does it involve?

Most junior bush fire brigades concentrate on training kids to use the equipment and, of course, fight fires. There may also be competitions between junior brigades at a local or state level.

You won't be called out to actually fight a fire until you become a full member at 17 but of course if the fire comes to you, and your home is threatened, it's not a bad idea to know what to do. (All too often local bush fire brigades are called out to distant fires and then fire threatens their own area while they are away. In cases like this, then it's good if EVERYONE knows the basics of firefighting.)

How do you go about it?

Not all bush fire brigades/country fire service brigades have junior members, even when the state organisation has a provision for it, but if you're interested or, even better, if you and a group of friends are interested, give your local brigade a ring and tell them. If you show interest, someone is pretty sure to decide it's time for a junior brigade!

In Victoria you can join a junior brigade if you are between 11–15. Apply to your local bush fire brigade, or call the CFA on (03) 9262 8444 or look up http://www.cfa.gov.au.

In New South Wales you can be a Firefly from 6–12, or a Cadet, or Junior Bush Fire Brigade member from 12–16. At the moment it is all fairly informally organised by local brigades, but there are plans within the next year to do a lot more in this area. You can also look up http://www.bushfire.nsw.gov.au or call the head office on (02) 9684 4411.

Tasmania doesn't have a coordinated junior bush fire programme (or didn't at the time of enquiring anyway) but they suggested that, if you are interested, to contact your local bush fire brigade.

In Western Australia there are no junior bush fire brigades, but there is a wonderfully coordinated programme run by the Department of Youth and Community Services, called Leadership W.A. See page 187.

In South Australia the country fire service brigades accept cadet members between the ages of 11–16. There are about 1000 cadets in South Australia, and they attend burn-offs, learn about hydrants, ladders and other equipment, how to operate the radio, read maps and do first aid. It's all run by the local brigades, so if you're interested, contact your local country fire services brigade. Even if they don't have cadets (some groups are really overextended — it's all voluntary — and just don't have the time) they may consider starting a programme if they know there are kids interested — after all, you're the fire heroes of tomorrow!

Queensland doesn't have a junior bush fire programme yet, but they are working on it, so it's worthwhile ringing the Queensland Fire and Rescue Unit. (Look it up in the phone book or ask directory assistance — the first number I was given was out of date, so I won't give you the number I finally got through on, in case they move office often!) Ask them if a programme has started yet.

In the Northern Territory there are no junior bush fire brigades, but you can join the Junior Rangers or the Junior Police Rangers (see page 186).

The volunteer bush fire brigades in the ACT may also have Junior brigade members, who learn all the basic skills of firefighting, equipment, first aid and radio. Contact your local volunteer bush fire brigade to see if they run a programme.

What will it cost?

Usually nil or very low.

Danger level

As a junior bush fire member, low. As an adult member, medium to deadly — every year volunteer bush fire fighters lose their lives (and every year the government expects these volunteers to do more and more).

Where can you go from here?

Most junior bush fire brigade members/fire service cadets go on to become volunteer bush fire fighters. When you are 16 or over you might also consider joining the State Emergency Service. These have different names in each state, but you can find them in the phone book by looking up emergency services.

These play an enormously important role in helping with disasters like the Thredbo landslide, floods or cyclones, or searching for people who are lost or attending vehicle accidents. You will learn everything from abseiling to first aid.

It's definitely challenging — often horrific — work, but if you have the courage and dedication, then you too can be one of Australia's volunteer heroes.

CHALLENGES FOR WHEN YOU'RE BROKE

➤ Join a club — bushwalking, rock climbing, surf lifesavers, or any of a few hundred others (pages 7–76).

➤ Go camping (page 20).

➤ Take public transport to the beach, river, lake, to swim, surf, wander or even make a raft out of a few hundred milk containers. (Except, yes, I know sometimes public transport can break the bank.)

➤ Bushwalk — find out where you might go from your local library, and take public transport to the starting point. (This is going to limit your destinations, but there are, almost certainly, still some to choose from.)

➤ Take the family WWOOFing. Even though you have to pay for membership, you won't have to pay for food while you are WWOOFing. (It's about the cheapest holiday you can have.) See page 162.

➤ Go fossicking.

➤ Go down to the library and get out a swag of books — not just stories, but books about how to do things (and you may even find something that will help you make some money). Libraries are free!

➤ Most libraries also have computers with Internet access that you can use, although you usually have to pay a small amount for this.

THE ARTS
(DRAMA, WRITING,
MUSIC . . . STUFF LIKE THAT)

DRAWING, SCULPTURE
PAINTING, PHOTOGRAPHY

The WOW factor

Creating something beautiful — or so real and vivid that you feel like crying — can be the greatest buzz there is.

Who would be interested?

Anyone who has determination and/or talent — even if you'll never be a professional, you will always have the joy of creating.

What does it involve?

That depends on your level of enthusiasm — anything from a short holiday course to passionately practising and refining your style.

How do you go about it?

As well as privately run courses, many schools organise after-school drawing and painting groups under supervision. Some schools also have darkroom facilities and most towns, and all cities, will have some sort of community photography club where members can access darkrooms and use equipment that would otherwise be prohibitively expensive. In Sydney the Australian Centre for Photography runs workshops and darkroom facilities for members, as does Photo Access in Canberra.

The various art schools in larger centres also run night-time courses which welcome younger people and can instruct you in drawing, painting, sculpture, photo-media, ceramics, glass, wood, metal — you name it. Again, look up 'Art Schools' in your local *Yellow Pages*. For any kid who is contemplating going to art school after the HSC, these classes give a fantastic taste of what you might find, so you can go and see if it is for you. Also ask your school's art teacher if they know of any clubs or courses in your district ... often they may know of one, but haven't mentioned it because they don't realise anyone is interested ... or they may know someone who knows someone who can find out!

Where can you go from here?

You can become a professional in all those areas, and there are tertiary courses in all of them.

FORM YOUR OWN CLUB

➤ If you're interested in some activity — whether it's rock climbing, bushwalking or embroidering budgies on your socks — it might be worthwhile forming a club at your school of people with the same interest.

➤ Once you have got a decent group of people together, you will be in a much better position to ask teachers and other adults if they would help you organise walks or other events and help you raise fund for equipment. It would also mean that parents can 'car pool' to take you to where you need to go — one parent can take the mob one week, another the next.

➤ Forming a club also shows adults you are serious about it, and not going to lose all interest by next Tuesday. It's also fun to be part of a group with the same interests, and work together on the same projects.

AMATEUR THEATRE

Amateur theatre is where most people involved have other jobs; they do their work at the theatre for nothing (because they love doing it) or for a very small wage. 'Professional' theatre is where everyone is paid a wage, and it's their main form of income.

The WOW factor

You will (eventually) find yourself in front of an audience who expect to be entertained, entranced and taken into another world, and who will applaud you if you make it happen. Or you might become part of the small army of people who help to make the magic happen — the scenery painters, the costume designers, the lighting technicians, the programme designers, the front-of-house staff, the props organisers, the scene changers, make-up artists . . .

What does it involve?

Most junior theatre groups run acting classes — you will learn basic acting techniques, make up, lighting, etc. Some amateur theatre groups put on 'junior' productions; others will have parts for kids in adult plays. (If you do get a role in an adult play, you will probably have to share it with someone else, so that you won't have to be on stage every night and get overtired.)

Who would be interested?

Anyone who likes acting, dressing up, and people who enjoy the drama of situations.

Theatre is also good for anyone who wants to learn how to 'project' themselves — how not to panic in front of an audience. If you are vaguely thinking you might like to work in TV, or be a barrister, teacher, sales representative, or do any job that involves convincing other people — or if you think you might want to be a writer — you might find the techniques that you would learn in amateur theatre useful.

I was involved with amateur theatre for years, and it's helped me enormously with my writing. (I learnt to 'think' myself into a character, which is a very valuable tool for writing.) But it also helped me learn how to give a speech in front of an audience and, of course, the techniques have been useful for me on *Burke's Backyard* too.)

How do you go about it?

Most major cities have at least one amateur theatre company — look up 'Theatres' in the *Yellow Pages* of the phone book. You may have to ring around a bit to see which group, if any, has a 'junior theatre' section — but quite possibly the first place you ring will be able to give you quite a lot of information. Most people who are involved in theatre will be really helpful once they find out that you are interested, and may tell you who to try next.

You will need to be able to:

- Turn up regularly for rehearsals, which may be after school, at night or on the weekend.
- Turn up on time to all performances … so you will need a cooperative adult handy who'll transport you, unless it's all reachable by public transport and during daylight hours.

What will it cost?

Anywhere from nothing to about $180 a term, so do ask about costs before you join. But if you are very, very keen, and your family can't or won't pay for you, I think it's a fairly good bet that if you have a talk with the person in charge before you start, they will work something out with you.

Danger level

Low; audiences rarely throw tomatoes nowadays (though my niece did develop an allergy to stage makeup but that's another story …).

Where can you go from here?

If you have the talent, passion and dedication, you can study at NIDA (National Institute of Dramatic Art) in Sydney, or similar organisations in other states, when you leave school — other colleges and universities offer dramatic arts, and courses in costume design, etc.

And then you can become an actor/actress, director or producer (not to mention learning which is which), costume designer, lighting director, director of photography, sound technician, musical opera star ...

There are, of course, also paid roles for kids in TV (especially advertisements) and theatre. Look up 'Theatrical Agents' in the *Yellow Pages* index.

Even if you aren't interested in acting — and have no wish whatsoever to make a fool of yourself on stage — you may possibly be interested in stage lighting, props, stage makeup, or just general theatre management.

Most kids who join amateur theatres want to act, but if you tell the people in charge that you are interested in other aspects of the theatre, they may just know someone who would like a helping hand, and who may be able to teach you a lot.

P.S. Many kids (and adults too of course) make a useful sum of money, or even their living, modelling. While adult models usually have to be thin and gorgeous, young models just have to be cute, attractive, and outgoing. Models can model clothes in shopping displays and fashion launches, but there is also a lot of work just being photographed for catalogues and advertisements in the newspaper or on TV.

If you think you've got a bright and bubbly personality (or you can fake one on stage) and the sort of grin that will sell a thousand swimming cossies, look up 'Modelling Agencies' in the *Yellow Pages*. It can be a very useful part-time job!

SINGING

The WOW factor

Learning to use your voice like a musical instrument, either by yourself, or as part of a team.

Who would be interested?

Anyone who loves music. ANYONE can sing, once they're shown how to do it. (But some people definitely sing better than others.)

How do you go about it?

You can learn singing by taking private lessons (and, yes, even if you do sound great when you sing now, singing lessons will make an extraordinary difference to the quality of your voice).

You can also join a choir. The singing lesson aspect won't be as intensive as it would be if you took private lessons, but you will learn the basics. Joining a good choir with an inspirational leader has enormous advantages, even if you have your heart and vocal cords set on a solo career. Your ability to read music will improve dramatically, the opportunities to perform will be arranged for you, you will be exposed to different types of music and some choirs regularly make CDs and even tour overseas. These opportunities open up faster for a well-organised and musically ambitious choir than they do for most solo performers.

Keep your eye on the newspapers, and when you see a youth choir is raising money for their tour of Italy take note of the name and make contact. You will probably have to audition (horrors!) and you will have to be committed to regular rehearsals as well as extra practise time at home, but in exchange you will have wonderful life experiences, make an army of friends and become familiar with the world of music and performers.

Look up 'Music', 'Bands', and 'Youth Activities' in the *Yellow Pages*. You should find several choirs, including youth choirs. Many churches, and all cathedrals, also have choirs — and, no, mostly you don't have to be a member of the church to join.

What will it cost?

Private singing lessons cost from about $30 per half hour or hour and upwards. Most choirs have a small membership fee, usually to cover the cost of sheet music and photocopying (about $10 a term), but some are free.

Danger level

Low.

Where can you go from here?

Music scholarships — including for voice — are available from conservatoriums of music, if you decide you want to use your voice professionally. You can also study to be a singing teacher, or you could decide that you just want to be semi-professional; i.e. sing in amateur productions but have another job to earn your keep.

If you think other people would pay to hear you sing, or you've formed a good singing group, look up 'Miscellaneous Agents' in the *Yellow Pages* of the phone book, and see if they can book you for parties, or weddings, or just take up busking — either by yourself or, better still, with a group of friends! In most places you need a licence to busk — if you think you are up to it, call your local council to ask where and when busking is permitted. And check with your parents too! It may be terrifying the first time you try it — but it can be a great way to get some money for Christmas.

PLAYING A MUSICAL INSTRUMENT

The WOW factor
Music, music, music.

Who would be interested?
People who love music. ANYONE can play an instrument — it's just a matter of finding the one that suits you. The drums? Trombone? Irish bagpipes? Electric guitar? Do you want to play rock music, jazz, folk music, or join a show band or a youth orchestra?

How do you go about it?
Choose the sort of music that moves you most (even if it's not what your friends or family like).

After that, well, if your parents are willing to pay for it, you can take music lessons (look up 'Music Teachers' in the *Yellow Pages*). If you want to be a professional musician, you need to keep studying — but if you want to play just for your own pleasure, after a few months or years (depending on the type of instrument you choose) you will know enough to be able to keep practising yourself.

School bands are also places to learn at least the basics of music, and many are much more sophisticated than that. Most schools with any well-integrated music programme will have a series of bands that you can work your way through, starting with novice level bands for beginners and culminating in performance bands which play in exciting venues (the interval at grand final football matches, the opening of Parliament, for Christmas pageants and local festivals).

The other huge advantage of playing in a band or orchestra is that many of us do not have the necessary self-discipline to practise without a specific goal, and the rehearsal and performance schedule will do that for you. Also, if you are nervous about public performance, this is the perfect way to conquer your nerves — in the company of others. Some Police Youth Clubs also have music training.

If you already play an instrument you can join a Youth Orchestra, or form your own band, string quartet, or join a folk music club. Look up the *Yellow Pages* of your local phone book under 'Clubs — Music' or 'Music' and 'Youth Activities'.

What will it cost?

Music lessons cost about $20 an hour upwards.

Danger level

Low, physically anyway — playing in public can be terrifying till you get used to it, though.

Where can you go from here?

Professional musicians play in orchestras and bands that are hired for concerts, parties, and pubs. But most musicians play for their own pleasure and that of their friends, or in community bands, with folk music clubs, or for dramatic societies. You can also study to be a music teacher or to teach music as occupational therapy for people with physical or mental problems. Some schools and conservatoriums of music also give music scholarships — your school would be the best place to find out about these (try the careers guidance counsellor or the librarian).

FOLK MUSIC CLUBS
AND FOLK DANCING

The WOW factor

No, don't think that this is too old-fashioned … get a taste of it first. Folk music is a type of music that has survived hundreds, or even thousands of years — and it has to be pretty catchy to do that. How much of today's music will still be played or sung in one hundred years time?

Folk music is also usually fun, very energetic — and it's a great place to meet people. (If you were swept away by the music of Riverdance, then maybe folk music is for you! And that was just Irish music … every culture in the world has their own music of the heart, and all of them have enough passion and rhythm to have survived.)

Who would be interested?

Anyone who likes music … and is open minded enough to like different sorts of music.

What does it involve?

At folk music clubs you'll listen to people sing and play instruments — anything from the balalaika to the Irish bagpipes, zither, mandolin, harp or guitar. (If you don't know what any of them are, pop along and find out.)

You will also get the chance to sing and play yourself, if you want to, either solo or with others.

Folk dancing is usually separate from folk music clubs. Sometimes it's associated with a particular national club; sometimes it's just done for fun. We used to have cleidahs in our local town. Cleidahs are Scottish dance and music nights — they were fast and fun and furious, with an enormous amount of sweat and laughter. Most of the people who went weren't Scottish at all, but everyone was welcome.

You will find that most folk music clubs are like that — even if you don't have any connection at all with the area the folk dances come from, people will be flattered that you're interested.

How do you go about it?

Look up 'Clubs' and 'Societies' in the *Yellow Pages* of the phone book for folk music clubs and folk dancing clubs. Many newspapers have a 'what's on' column where the club's activities will be mentioned. Sometimes looking at the advertisements on the notice board at your local library can find them too.

Age limit

The clubs are mostly for adults, but folk dancing and folk music are areas where kids are really welcomed — you will probably find other young people there already. If you are a little nervous about going, convince a friend to go too.

What will it cost?

Most clubs have a small membership fee, just to cover costs, but often you can go along for a few visits before you have to join — and if you really can't afford it, just say so!

Where can you go from here?

Music is something that can stay with you all your life, but there are professional folk musicians too. They may not quite have the celebrity status of rock stars, but some are famous around the world, and if you are good enough, dedicated — and very lucky — you might be able to make your living at it too.

WRITING STORIES, BOOKS, POETRY

The WOW factor

See the worlds in your head become a story, or the images become a poem. And see your work published, then have other people actually buy it and read it ...

How do you go about it?

The best way to become a writer is just to write and write and be critical of your writing; and to read as much as you possibly can, because that will teach you the techniques of writing.

But if you want some help along the way, you could try your local Writers Centre (look it up the phone book) — there is one in each capital city, and in many regional centres.

They will have details of magazines where you can submit work to be published, writing workshops and books about writing. Most of these will be for adults, but you will be able to glean some useful bits and there is no reason why you can't front up to a writing workshop that's mostly for adults.

I've given lots of writing workshops for adults where the occasional kid has turned up. No one has minded, because the kids concerned were enthusiastic and certainly not bored by spending a whole day just writing and talking about writing.

On the other hand, I've given workshops where parents have pushed their 'brilliant' kids into joining — and the kids have been bored stiff after a few hours. If you're a kid reading this and you feel like going for an adult workshop — more power to you. If you're a parent reading this, please don't send your kid to an adult workshop, no matter how brilliant you think they are. If it's not their own idea, chances are they'll hate it.

You may be a bit out of your depth at times if you are a kid in an adult writing workshop, but if you are really seriously thinking about becoming a writer, working with adults will give you a more realistic idea of how far you need to go for your work to be good enough to publish, rather than just comparing it to stuff from other school kids.

Another good place to contact is the Australian Society of Authors ... you probably won't want to join until you're an adult, and seriously into becoming a professional writer, but you could look up their website on http://www.asauthors.org or you can write to them at P.O. Box 1566, Strawberry Hills, NSW 2012. The A.S.A. has details of competitions, some of which have a young writers' category, and they also run mentorships for writers who are just beginning, which is where a writer who is just starting out is paired with a more experienced writer. These mentorships are for adults, not kids, but it's useful to know that one might be available for you in a few years time!

You might also think about forming a writers' group at school — kids like yourself who are serious about writing. You can talk about books, swap places where you might get a story or poem published, even criticise each other's work if you are brave enough. Have a chat to your school librarian too — the library is often a good place to start. Your librarian will probably know of the nearest place that regularly gives writing workshops for kids, either day workshops, or ones that last weekends or even longer.

If your school librarian isn't interested, or your school doesn't have a full-time librarian, you could also have a chat to the head librarian at your local library, to see if they can offer some useful suggestions. Librarians are people who are really into books and reading, and even if it isn't part of their job, they may be good people to point you in a fascinating direction.

There are also writing camps organised during school holidays which (depending on who is running them) can be a wonderfully intense way of engaging with your own writing amongst equally passionate people.

Usually they are organised to allow contemplation and writing time during the day and in the evening people read and comment on their own, and each other's, efforts. When well handled, this can be a time when you make real progress with your writing, whether it is poetry or prose. Most of these camps send information to local schools, but your school may not think that it's worthwhile to pass it on unless they know there are kids who are really interested. Ask!

There are also sites on the Internet where you can publish your own work ... these change almost weekly, so I haven't included any here. Ask your school librarian if they can give you any pointers! Your school library will also have copies of magazines with kid's contributions in them. Again, ask your librarian! If they don't know, they will know how to find out.

What will it cost?

Advice will probably cost zilch, and most people will give you help for free. Writing workshops, though, can cost from about $20 to $100 a day, depending on who's giving them, and also whether they are 'live-in' courses — where food and accommodation has to be paid for too. And of course, forming your own writers' or reading group won't cost anything either ... you can get your books from the library!

Danger level

Low — writers are sometimes nice civilised people and most only rarely turn into werewolves before midnight.

Where can you go from here?

Yes, it is possible to make a living being a writer, if you're good enough and persevere ... and the sooner you start really working at it, the sooner you'll get there.

FM COMMUNITY RADIO

The WOW factor

You will be part of that wonderful world of media.

Who would be interested?

Anyone interested in either the on-air side, or the technical areas, of radio.

What does it involve?

Most areas are served by at least one FM radio station (as well as the main commercial and ABC radio stations) and these are often run by a community group, or even several community groups. They sometimes (although not always, by any means) run courses for people interested in working in radio, either on air, or in various technical areas. Also, they are sometimes (but again not always) grateful for volunteers to do anything from researching stories to making cups of coffee and sweeping the floor. You may even be given the chance to do your own thing on air, if you can come up with a decent programme idea. But be prepared to be given a slot in the wee small hours, or during the afternoon doldrums — you are unlikely to crack the breakfast slot, the afternoon shift or the early evening, which are maximum audience times — to begin with.

How do you go about it?

Look up 'Radio Stations' in the *Yellow Pages* of the phone book and ring up any that have FM as part of their name, and ask if they are community radio stations. Or just say that you are interested in radio and ask if they have any role for volunteers or trainees at their station. Some of the FM stations will be commercial ones (i.e. ones staffed by professionals) but the receptionist at one of those should be able to tell you what the community stations in your area — if they happen to be feeling obliging (and if you sound like an eager, polite kid they are more likely to be suddenly feeling helpful).

Commercial and ABC radio stations sometimes offer work experience through schools, but be prepared for knock backs — there are many kids who want work experience, and there are just not enough radio people to go round.

What will it cost?

Low; some community radio stations have membership fees; others will charge for their workshops.

Danger level

Low, unless you do extremely idiotic things with wires and cables.

Where can you go from here?

Community radio is a great experience if you are considering a job in professional radio or TV — either on-air or as a producer, researcher or technician.

CREATIVE GRAFFITI
(COMMUNITY ART)

The WOW factor

Seeing your artwork or political comments in public, where they can be admired or inspire people — or at least make them think.

Who would be interested?

Anyone who has a talent for art, or has something they want to say to society.

What does it involve?

No, I am NOT encouraging you to go and spray paint the local shopping centre ... well, yes I am, but this is how you do it legally, so that you don't get hauled off by the police or stuck with a community service order for the next umpteen weekends. This way you will have time to actually do the job properly, instead of scampering off if someone approaches.

How do you go about it?

Step 1. Work out what sort of graffiti you want to do ... do you just want to use a graffiti wall to put down your thoughts about life, death, and politicians, or do you want to create public art ... something beautiful or inspiring?

(A graffiti wall is one where anyone can write any slogans or limericks they like. Every month or so they are painted over so people can write more stuff on them.)

Step 2. Work out where you would like to put it.

Good places to choose are the sidings, or temporary fences, around major building sites. Because they will eventually get taken down, it's fairly easy to get permission to use them.

Other places where councils may give permission for 'public art' include wide concrete bridge supports, bus shelters, the walls of public toilets (both inside and out) and sometimes even trams or buses.

The more organised and beautiful your work is, the more likely it is that you are going to be able convince the council to give you the space to create it.

Step 3. Convince a few helpful adults to go to bat for you ... to convince the council that you are serious and committed, and that the public will just love what you are going to do — cheer their busy lives up for them for nothing!

Good people to start with are your art teacher, other teachers, parents, and anyone involved in activities for kids i.e. Scouts or church youth clubs. The local police could also be approached ... point out that if kids have somewhere they can legally splash paint about, they will be less likely to do it illegally.

Step 4. Come up with a really detailed plan of what you are planning to create.

Step 5. Convince the council (some councils are much easier to convince that others).

Step 6. Go to it!

What will it cost?

You may have to buy the paint ... on the other hand, you may find a really generous council that will pay for it ... or you can ask a local hardware store to sponsor the event, and donate the paint. (Then ring up the local paper, TV or radio station and tell them what's on and when, so that the sponsor gets some publicity in return!)

Where can you go from here?

There are many careers in art; I have friends whose main work is creating public murals — great big paintings for public areas that take up a whole wall or even more, mostly for hospitals, libraries, swimming pools and so forth.

HOME-MADE
ADVENTURES

COLLECTING HISTORY

The WOW factor

Most of us live in a little box called the present, but even within living memory life has been very different (and even during your lifetime, the way we live will change even more).

Who would be interested?

Anyone who likes people, stories and history.

What does it involve?

One of the best ways to learn about history is to talk to the people who were there. ANY person over, say 50, will be able to tell you about a very different way of life from now and they will also be able to tell you what it was like to live through the Second World War or the Vietnam War, the 'hippy' sixties and seventies and much more, whether they grew up in Australia or have incredible stories to tell you from overseas.

How do you go about it?

Collecting people's stories is called collecting 'oral history'. Contact your local museum — they may run courses on collecting oral history, or they may have an oral history project that you can help with. Often this just involves using a tape recorder and asking interesting questions to get the person being interviewed going.

What will it cost?

Low to nil.

Danger level

Low — as long as you don't just charge off on your own into strange people's houses and start asking questions.

Where can you go from here?

You might decide to become an historian, archaeologist or museum curator.

FINDING TREASURE
(GOLD AND JEWELS)

The WOW factor

Money, money, money — and somehow gold and jewels are even more exciting than their money equivalent.

Who would be interested?

Anyone.

What does it involve?

There are many areas of Australia where you can fossick in creeks, and you might just find a trace of gold, or where you can hunt for gems or semi-precious stones.

To be honest, your chances of making it rich are about zilch, but you may still come up with a few pretty bits and pieces. (A couple of fossickers used to camp on the old gold fields around here for their holidays each year. It took them about twenty years to fossick enough gold to make a ring for each of them but, as they said, they had great fun doing it.) In some areas of Australia you might just find a gold nugget by using a metal detector (metal detectors can be hired). You might also find tin cans, lost and defunct watches and loose change — just don't get your hopes up too much and you should have fun.

Do make sure you either have the landowner's permission to be on their land, or that you are in a designated fossicking area. Also, be aware of soil erosion issues and don't leave horrible great holes or acres of disturbed soil behind, and pick up your rubbish. If you turn up pieces of metal that are potentially dangerous to stock, use your scone and clear up after yourself.

P.S. My son went fossicking for semi-precious stones a few years ago. He brought back a few very, very pretty little bits, which I took to a jewellery shop to get polished and then made into jewellery. It's not valuable, but it's great to have and has a lot of good memories attached.

How do you go about it?

Go to the library and look up books on fossicking, gold and semi-precious stones. (The librarian can help you find them — the books that is ... sadly you hardly ever turn up gold and jewels on library shelves ... but you never know your luck.) They should tell you some of the areas where you might start searching — and how to go about it.

Another good way of starting is to ring up the tourist bureau in your state and ask about fossicking or gem-hunting tours. These are usually well organised and you'll learn the basics of what to look for — what they look like in their raw (i.e. dirty) state, and how to go about getting it out of the dirt and into your hands.

You can also contact your state Department of Mines, and just hope they have a helpful information section. (Sometimes government information sections can be wonderful; sometimes they've all gone to lunch and don't bother ringing back, or just say vaguely, 'We don't know anything about that'.) Most Departments of Mines have pamphlets about fossicking areas in their state, and sometimes useful websites too.

Queensland

If you live in Queensland the place you need to contact is the Queensland Department of Mining and Energy (http://www.dme.qld.gov.au/resdev/landuse/fossick/gtq. htm).

Licences are available from the district offices of the Department of Mines and Energy and local agents, including local governments and businesses.

There are also designated fossicking lands, where the government has negotiated the landowners' permission in advance. If you want a list of fossicking sites, look up http://www.dme.qld.gov.au/resdev/landuse/fossick/dfl. htm ... you'll find places where there are sapphire and zircon gems, alluvial gold in creeks, topaz, tin, quartz crystal and cassiterite, agates, chalcedony and thunder eggs, citrine, smoky quartz and aquamarine, opals, diamonds, petrified wood, peridot and lots of other stuff — and the website will also tell you if you can camp there or what other accommodation is available. (P.S. if you have any spare petrified wood, send some to me — I love the stuff!!!)

Western Australia

If you're in Western Australia, look up http://www.dme. wa.gov.au/prodserv/pub/mining_info/2.html or contact the Western Australia Department of Minerals and Energy.

In Western Australia, a Miner's Right may be obtained for a fee of $20 at the Department of Minerals and Energy (Mineral House, 100 Plain Street, East Perth) or at any Mining Registrar's Office.

Northern Territory

If you're in the Northern Territory (or plan to visit there) contact the Northern Territory Visitors Centre. Try looking up http://www.northernterritory.com/6-1-12.html.

The Northern Territory is an incredible area for gem fossicking. You'll find (or at least can look for) agate, amethyst, apatite, peridot, beryl, garnet, gold, jaspar, magnetite, mica, microline, pyrite, quartz, ribbonstone, tourmaline and zircon.

Most of the gem fossicking areas are located around Central Australia. You can either follow the advice in pamphlets and maps from the Tourist Commission, or you can join a fossicking tour like Norm's Gold and Scenic Tours out of Tennant Creek, or Gun Alley Gold Panning in Pine Creek. Or you can go to famous Gemtree, east of Alice Springs, which has accommodation, hire equipment, expert guides, gem cutting services and Tag-a-long tours. Tours usually depart daily, include an experienced guide and all fossicking equipment, and you can also watch tour-associated gem cutters turn your stones into beautifully faceted gems.

Fossicking tours, including a guide, equipment and stone evaluation, costs about $40 per set of equipment which can be used by one to four people.

New South Wales

If you're in New South Wales contact the NSW Department of Mineral Resources or look up http://www.minerals.nsw.gov.au/mapspubs/publish/minfacts/05.htm.

With the introduction of the Mining Act, 1992, fossicking licences are no longer required to go fossicking in NSW, and there is no fee payable. You can fossick anywhere in the state — providing certain conditions are met. Check out the website for details. Keep in mind, though, that to fossick you do need to get the landowner's permission, or the permission of the person who holds the mineral exploration licence, unless the land is within a fossicking district. Contact the Department of Mineral Resources for a list.

Good places to hunt for treasure in NSW include The Fossicker's Way, New England, and the North West Slopes. Look for alluvial gold and precious stones like zircons, sapphires, chrysoprase, serpentine and crystals. Also try fossicking in Tamworth and Bingara (marble, garnets, jasper, petrified wood, fossils and even a coral reef are all in the district). A detailed brochure of the fossicking areas is available from the Visitors Centre.

Inverell has numerous areas for people to fossick. You may find sapphires, zircon, quartz, soap stone, topaz, diamonds, tourmaline, tin and various others. Some of the roadside creeks have small zircons and garnets, which show up on a fine sieve.

There are also lots of other places. Just look them up! (We have an area for gold fossicking near us, but be warned — so many people go through it every year that unless there has just been a flood, which brings more gold down, you probably won't find much!)

Victoria

If you're in Victoria look up http://www.vic.gov.au. You'll need to buy a Miner's Right, which costs $18 for 2 years. There are many places you can get them including most visitors centres in the areas where you are likely to find gold, and stores that specialise in prospecting and metal detectors.

There are also fossicking areas in the Otway National Park (gemstones), Mornington Peninsula National Park (gemstones), Cape Liptrap Coastal Park (gemstones), Steiglitz Historic Park, Beechworth Historic Park, Kara Kara State Park, Kooyoora State Park, Kamarooka State Park, Whipstick State Park, Paddy's Ranges State Park and Enfield State Park.

Contact Parks Victoria on 13 19 63 if you want more information.

Tasmania

In Tasmania there are great places to fossick.

Derby, in the north-east, was founded on the tin-mining industry, and there is now a fascinating mining museum there. There is also a local tour to the best spots to fossick for gems. At Winnaleah, north of Derby, you can fossick for sapphire, topaz, zircon, black spinel, chrysoberyl and alexandrite — you might find a stone good enough to have set in a ring.

The topaz found on Flinders Island is called locally 'Killiecrankie diamond'. Local people are usually happy to point out the best fossicking spots, and there are also fossicking tours.

In the south of Tasmania, near Lune River, fossickers often find agate and pieces of fossilised wood.

South Australia

If you want to go fossicking in South Australia, there are some rewarding places to go. Ask at your local visitor information centre to see if there's an area you *don't* need a licence to fossick in South Australia. As long as you only use metal detectors, gold pans or picks and shovels — no machinery allowed! For more details, look up the Department of Minerals and Energy at: http://www.pir.sa. gov.au/pages/minerals/legislation/faq-fossick.htm.

What will it cost?

Very low — apart from the cost of getting to the right place to start searching. A gold panning dish costs about $10, but you can just use a bowl or a sieve if you don't have one. A Miner's Right or Fossicking Licence costs about $20, but most states have areas where you can fossick without one. Fossicking tours start from about $20 for an hour's demonstration to between $40 and $120 a day.

If you want to hire a metal detector, they cost about $20 per 24-hour day during the week, and $25 at the weekends and on public holidays, plus about a $20 deposit. Super detectors start at about $40, and then go up to $60 and $70 per day with $200 deposit, and there are packages and weekly rates too. Most places that hire or sell metal detectors also run courses on how to use them, which is a lot more necessary than most people realise! They may also offer courses on prospecting and fossicking, which again, are fairly essential if you've never done it before.

A new metal detector will cost thousands of dollars, but you may be able to buy a second-hand one for hundreds. Ask at specialty stores that sell metal detectors and fossicking equipment — look them up in the *Yellow Pages*.

Danger level

Low — apart from sunburn.

Where can you go from here?

You could study geology at university; or become a professional gem hunter, searching for opals or other gems; or study lapidary and learn to polish them and put them in jewellery. There are still people who fossick for a living, hunting for precious and semi-precious stones.

WORKING ON ORGANIC FARMS (WWOOFING!)

This is another challenge where you do have to drag an adult along with you, but if you're persuasive enough you should be able to get one interested ... or even fascinated. (Try your teacher if your parents give you the thumbs down.)

The WOW factor

Have you ever wondered what it's like working on a real farm or how people actually build their own houses from mud, bricks or stone, or build their own power systems — solar, wind or waterwheels? Can you really grow all your own food or build your own house for a few hundred dollars?

With WWOOF (Willing Workers on Organic Farms) you will learn how people actually grow things without using harmful chemicals, and how they build their own houses and power systems, or how to keep hens, cows and other livestock without battery or factory farming.

Who would be interested?

Anyone interested in farming, growing things, animals, alternative power, building or just the outdoors — or even if you only want to get out of the city or the suburbs for a day or ten.

What does it involve?

Under the WWOOF Scheme people who are interested in volunteering to work on organic farms, for anywhere from a day to a few months, pay to receive a list of farms.

The list will tell you where the farm is, what sort of things are grown, whether they are also involved in, say, making mudbricks, or building a wind generator or drying herbs. The list will also tell you the sorts of jobs you might be doing — anything from shovelling manure to weeding or picking fruit — and what sort of accommodation and food you will get. (Some places have comfortable bedrooms; in other places you will be expected to bring your own tent.)

About a third of WWOOF farms don't take kids at all and about another third don't usually take kids, but are prepared to listen if you say that you are really interested. Some WWOOFers really love showing kids what a different life can be like!

You may have to assure both the farmers and your parents that, yes, you are prepared to work all day and, no, you won't whinge about the food, even if it's salad for lunch and you hate salad, and, no, you won't try and ride the horse in the far paddock without permission.

WWOOFing is hard work, but everyone I know who has done it has said that it was incredible fun and enormously interesting — you meet a range of people and do things you may otherwise never have dreamt of and there are plenty of places on the WWOOF list to choose from.

We used to belong to the WWOOF scheme here and we met a lot of wonderful people. Some just wanted a day out in the country, and were happy to do a few hours gentle weeding in exchange for lunch, a tour round the place and a basket of home grown fruit at the end of the day. Others came for a weekend, or even weeks. We had one WWOOFer stay for six months — he was a postgraduate agricultural student from Germany and he needed practical experience before he could get his degree. One of my favourite WWOOF stories is the 20-year-old who found out about the scheme accidentally. He'd been unemployed ever since he left school, and decided to go WWOOFing just for something to do. He went to a place where the owners were building their own mudbrick house, and two years later they got a letter from their WWOOFer, telling them how he and some friends had set up a business making mudbricks for houses. Business was booming and he was about to get married. (He'd just about finished building his own house too.)

How do you go about it?

Contact WWOOF Australia, Mt Murrindal Coop, Buchan, Victoria 3885 or phone/fax on (03) 5155 0218. You can also check out their website at: http://www.earthlink.com. au/wwoof. They will send you a list of farms and you can choose which ones you're interested in. You then ring them up, or write to them to see if there is a time you can visit them. (Although some farms get so many applications that they can't take them all.)

There are WWOOF farms all over Australia — sometimes they are large wheat farms, cattle farms or orchards, and sometimes they are just large city blocks, where the owners grow most of their own food. You can get to some of the farms by public transport (or the owners may be prepared to come and pick you up from a nearby town). With most farms though, it's much easier if you can drive there.

Some farms, especially those near cities, often have WWOOFers coming out for just one day; in other places you can stay for a weekend, or even weeks or months.

What will it cost?

A single membership costs $35, a couple membership costs $40. There are no kids' or family memberships, as kids aren't covered by the scheme's insurance, so if you choose to go WWOOFing you will have to do it at your own risk until you are 17.

Danger level

Low — as long as you remember to wear decent boots, a good hat, work gloves, be cautious with animals and don't fiddle with farm machinery by yourself. But farms can be very dangerous places if you are not sensible. (Farming is actually one of the most dangerous occupations in Australia.)

Where can you go from here??

You can WWOOF all over Australia — in other words, just go from farm to farm, working a few days at one and a few weeks at another. It's a great way to see the country. Even if you are not paid, you don't have to pay for your accommodation and food. You can also join overseas WWOOFing organisations, and see even more of the world. (And if you are interested in studying agriculture or ecology, WWOOFing can be an incredible education.)

WWOOFing can also teach you that, yes, it IS possible to build your own house or power system and, yes, you can grow most of your own food and not have to buy it, even on a largish city block.

JOIN A POLITICAL PARTY

The WOW factor

Ever felt that ordinary people don't really have much say in how the country is run, even when you do get to vote once you are over 18?

Well, you are pretty right but if you join a political party you will have a *much* greater voice when politicans are creating party policies. (Basically Australia is run by political parties and the people that belong to those parties decide the policy.)

What does it involve?

Most political parties have junior or youth sections where party policy is debated. Okay, the parties don't HAVE to take notice of what the junior members believe, but they are usually pretty influential — if only because it's really bad publicity if the junior group of whatever party is in government says that the government is behaving like a bunch of twits.

Junior groups of political parties are also involved in fundraising, campaigning, helping out at elections and there may be a fairly active social life too, with dances, barbecues and debates — and not just about political issues. This will vary, though, with each party. For example, the Greens youth division has discussion groups on the web.

How do you go about it?

You may already support a political party or you could look up 'Organisations — Political' in the *Yellow Pages* index and then ring up each party and ask them what they believe in and why. (This isn't always a good test though, because it will depend on the friendliness and eloquence of the person who happens to answer the phone at the other end, and sometimes political parties can sound really good, but aren't quite so hot when it comes to action.)

Once you have a list of a party or two that sound okay, read the newspapers and watch the news on TV for a few months to see how good they are in practice, and what other people say about them — both good and bad. And of course ask your parents, teachers and any other moderately intelligent adults you come across and take their views into account too.

Now look up the *Yellow Pages* again to get the number of the political party, say that you would like to join, and ask how you go about it. If there isn't a junior branch near you, you might also ask how to go about starting one up. Political parties depend on membership to survive, so you are pretty sure to find them really helpful.

Lots of political parties also have websites. You can look them up and get an idea of the ideals and beliefs of the different parties. Try the Labor Party at: http://www.alp.org.au, the Liberal party at: http://www.liberal.org.au, the Democrats at: http://www.democrats.org.au, the National Party at: http://www.npa.org.au and the Greens at: http://www.greens.org.au.

And if you decide to support a political party your parents hate, at least give them a chance to explain why they hate it, and then decide whether it might not be a good idea to wait a few years to consider the whole issue.

Also, you don't have to stay with the first party you choose. I have a friend who's been a member of the Liberal Party, the Democrats, and now the Labor Party — at least I think that's where he is now!

Age limit

You have to be between 15 and 26 for Young Labor; the Liberal Party and Australian Democrats Youth Groups and they generally have an upper age limit of 30. Anyone of any age can be a full member of the Greens, but they also run the Green Youth Network.

What will it cost?

Most political parties are organised state by state, or region by region, and mostly, each branch will set its own fees. It costs between about $20–$40 a year to join the Young Liberals, depending on which state you're in, $40 (or $20 concession) to join the Young Australia Democrats (or YADS), and membership for Young Labor varies according to region. For the Greens, if you don't have a regular income (pocket money *doesn't* count) it costs $5–$20 to join.

Where can you go from here?

Political youth groups are a great way to get experience — and political friends — if you are interested in a career in politics, either as a politician (in federal, state or local government), as a political adviser, party organiser or press secretary. Sadly, some people do join political parties because they think knowing the politicians in government might help them get public service jobs or government contracts.

But one of the best reasons for joining a political party is because the more people who are really concerned about how this country is run, the better it will be. Who was it who said that if evil is to flourish, all good men need to do is nothing?

HUNTING FOR THINGUMMIES

No, not exploring to Timbuctoo — sorry, that will have to wait a few years. Just exploring your own area.

No, it's not as boring as it sounds . . .

When I was your age, more or less, a gang of us decided that we would like to try green ice-cream. This was back in the dark ages, when ice-cream mostly came in white or brown or strawberry, but a friend of someone's sister's cousin, or something like that, said she'd once bought a green ice-cream at a particular shop so we decided to search for it.

This was in Brisbane, so we weren't exactly going on safari. We went by bus mostly, and trams (because there were still trams in those days) and we searched through just about every city street, and I don't know how many journeys it took us, but finally we did find the green ice-cream.

I can't remember what it tasted like — probably much like the white, brown or pink ice-cream, with maybe a bit of peppermint or lime added, but I do remember the fun of searching for it.

And that's what I learnt then — most of the fun of hunting for something is actually doing it, not finding the thing that you're looking for.

It doesn't really matter what you decide to look for. How do I know what you're interested in? But probably the sillier it is the better, and you do need a good gang to go with.

The WOW factor

Even in your own city or local area, it can be amazing how much of it will be new to you, and even if you've been there before via car and parents, it's different when you have done it yourself.

Who would be interested?

Anyone with a good group of friends who enjoy doing slightly eccentric things.

How do you go about it?

Choose the object of your hunt, get a map and work out places where it might be. Then work out how to go there, collect bus and train timetables (and whatever else you may need) and work out when you can get to where you want to go and how to get back again. And do let someone know where you are going and when and be prepared for them to giggle when you tell them why. (I bet they giggled at all the great explorers way back when.)

What will it cost?

Depends how much your local public transport system charges.

Danger level

Low, if you are sensible and have a back-up system in case you get stranded somewhere — that is, a parent to ring who will come and rescue you. And let them know your planned route, too.

Where can you go from here?

Well, maybe Timbuctoo …

BREAK A RECORD

The WOW factor

You become the world's greatest — even if it's only the world's greatest bubble blower or phone card collector or you have baked the largest cake in the world. (Don't even consider that one — the record is now so unbelievably large that unless you are thinking in tonnes and hectares you are not even in with a chance — but I haven't heard of anyone tackling, say, the largest chocolate crackle.)

Who would be interested?

Dunno. I've never been interested in breaking records, but there must be a lot of you out there or we wouldn't have the *Guinness Book of Records*.

How do you go about it?

Go to your library, get out the *Guinness Book of Records*, and either find something no one has thought of establishing a world record for, or choose something that you think you can do even better/faster/bigger/longer/more.

What will it cost?

Depends what you choose to do.

Danger level

Again, depends.

Where can you go from here?

Who knows? But at least the whole thing may be a giggle ... and you might even be able to gather sponsors and raise money for charity. (I'd sponsor anyone who was going to try to make the world's largest chocolate crackle!)

GO EXPLORING

All cities, towns, and country areas have buses wandering through them, and if you ask around you may be amazed exactly how far (and back) you can get in a day. A trip to the coast, or a far-off beach that you haven't seen before, or the snow country — all of these are possibilities.

Again, most of the pleasure will be in the getting there — you probably won't have much time before you have to come back.

The WOW factor

Getting there, finding out what it's like, and getting back.

Who would be interested?

Anyone with a touch of adventure or curiosity.

What does it involve?

Find out what forms of public transport are available — train, bus, or tram. Then find out how far they go and what their timetable is, and plan from there.

How do you go about it?

Your local city council should have details of public transport. Also look under 'Buses' in the *Yellow Pages* for private bus companies that the council may not know about.

What will it cost?

This depends on type of transport and distance.

Danger level

Low, as long as you keep to the timetable, tell your parents where you are going and when you are getting back and you don't do anything dumb (i.e. don't decide to hitch a ride instead), and always go in a group of three or four. If someone suspicious approaches you, YELL and call for help.

Where can you go from here?

Today: a short trip to the beach. Tomorrow: the mountains of Nepal. You could also form a dangerous addiction to travelling and peering into other people's lives.

DOING THINGS

What sort of things?

There will probably be places of great fascination in your area that you may not even have considered, like the local sewerage depot — no, don't groan … do you know how many diamond rings have been discovered at your local sewerage station? And how many really weird things that I really won't go into here, but you may find even more interesting? (But not crocodiles … the crocodiles in New York's sewerage system are a myth … but all sorts of other stuff goes down the sewers.) Many sewerage stations hold open days — and even if they don't, you may be able to arrange a tour.

Most areas have museums (sometimes several); many radio and TV stations have either open days or tours — or they will organise one if you show interest. Local recycling centres at the dump can be fascinating places to browse — and a really cheap place to get all sorts of stuff to make anything from a go-kart to a perpetual motion robot.

Most universities and technical colleges have open days, where they demonstrate all sorts of things — not just their lecture halls and residential colleges, etc., but things that wriggle or go bang, often with hands-on demonstrations as well.

Go and pay a visit to your local tourist board … often it's the people who live in an area that are the last to enjoy all sorts of stuff which tourists from other areas have already done!

The WOW factor

Many and various!

Who would be interested?

That depends on what's on … but there is sure to be something that will grab you, sometime or another.

How do you go about it?

Ask your local tourist board, or visitor information centre, for interesting things in your area and look in the local paper regularly in the 'what's on' section ... and generally keep your eyes open.

Is there a mysterious building on your way to school? Find out what it is ... and ask if you can have a tour. A surprising number of factories, businesses, radio stations, newspapers and so forth, will say yes ... and go to a lot of trouble to organise it for you.

(Just to be cautious, do tell your parents where you are going, just in case it's a factory staffed by aliens who plan to chop you up for fertiliser.)

What will it cost?

Should be about zilch, though you will have to get there and back.

MAKING SOMETHING

The WOW factor

There is incredible pleasure in creating something that never existed before your hands and brain made it happen.

Who would be interested?

Anyone — you just need to find the sort of things you would be interested in making.

What does it involve?

Make jewellery, pottery, take up woodcarving or blacksmithing (yes, there are still blacksmiths making stuff from metal), build a boat, or at least a raft (some kids around here built one from old plastic milk bottles strapped together — it even floated!), build a fountain (you can buy fountain kits from some garden centres), get a group together and make a friendship quilt (you knit or sew a few squares each, then sew them all together) and then raffle it for charity or make one for each of you!

There are a million, million projects you could do and you'll get some ideas from looking up books in the craft section at your local library — some books have very detailed plans and instructions — or glancing through magazines at the newsagents. (Many hobby magazines carry detailed instructions on particular projects.)

How do you go about it?

Research the project as carefully as you can — the time to do research is before you start, not during. (Except once you get enthused you won't pay any attention to this and you will dive in anyway. But at least I told you to.) Cost it out carefully. Can you really afford the materials? Can you really spend that long doing it? Should you be less ambitious, at least the first time? Then get to it!

Also, try looking up 'Clubs' and 'Societies' in the phone book, in case there's a whole mob of people interested in making the same sorts of things, or 'Crafts' in case someone is advertising lessons in, say, teddy bear making, or ultra-light aircraft construction.

What will it cost?

Will vary, depending on what you want to make and if you need specialist tools and materials.

Danger level

Depends whether you want to build a rocket or embroider a giant tablecloth. Most crafts are reasonably danger free, but there are the odd unexpected twists of fate — I once got stabbed through the wrist while I was woodcarving (luckily, I was sitting next to a doctor who was doing the same course) and some pottery glaze materials may be poisonous if you do not take care to follow instructions.

Where can you go from here?

As people gradually become tired of being able to buy only the same mass produced stuff in shops, more and more they are looking for things made by craftspeople. Everything from furniture to boats, houses, icecream, jewellery, pottery, quilts, or handmade dolls and teddy bears created with love and imagination. What's just a hobby today might become a full-time job in ten years time.

About getting to "come" and "stacked" at the bread basket, in case there's a warm prop "a great appetite" in making the same sort of things... Carbohydrates only if everything is kept up, so which page.

What will I eat?

Will eat, depending on when you want to make certain you read snacks for foods and bread.

Is it safe?

...

When can you get on track?

...

SCOUTS

Try their webpage http://www.scouts.com.au or call 1800 726 887 (a free call) and you will be put in touch with the head office in your state.

Just about every area has a Scout group, so they can be one of the best places to start for a whole range of activities. They are also very cheap to join (fees vary from area to area) and they are incredibly good value for money!

Scouts are separated into four groups by age — Joey Scouts for kids 6–8, Cub Scouts for boys and girls aged 8–11, Scouts for girls and boys aged between 10½–15, and then Venturers.

Kids in Scouts get to do a whole range of activities, depending pretty much on the skills and energy of the volunteer adults who run the local group, as well as how much energy and enthusiasm the kids in the group show for various activities. There is a lot of emphasis on camping, first aid, canoeing, sailing, orienteering, and outdoor cooking, as well as games and craft. If one troop doesn't seem to be doing the adventurous things you want, it is worth scouting around — no pun intended — to see if another group is more your cup of tea.

Sea Scouts, for example, are more into sea activities. If you've ever wanted to learn how to fly, Scouts even have their own Cessnas — but you have to be over 16 to learn how to fly them.

Scouts is a good place to start looking for adventurous activities. Some kids love Scouts; others find the activities too tame, and while the Scout leaders do have good basic training, they are very unlikely to be experts in all areas. (A Scout leader interested in sailing, for example, might only have the bare minimum of qualifications in abseiling.) But this can vary enormously — I would really recommend at least giving them a go.

Remember — if you want something more adventurous, or are really interested in sailing or abseiling — ASK!!! The people in Scouts will really try to help you do whatever challenges you. If you want more adventures — tell them! Or maybe you can convince more adventurous kids to join your local group.

VENTURERS

Venturers are for young women and men aged between 14 and 18.

There are usually about 15 people in a unit and, unlike Scouts, the Venturers have a lot of say in what they do and how they do it, through their own Unit Council.

Activities tend to be a lot more adventurous too — from sailing, skiing, exploring underwater reefs, and earning your pilot's licence, to editing your own films, or rock climbing; as well as dances, bushwalks, barbecues, and the like. Different Venturers groups tend to be into different things, depending on who's involved. Contact the Scout Association of Australia for your nearest group — or a selection of groups — to see who seems to be doing the sort of stuff you might like and at the level you are interested in. If one lot seems boring, try another!

THE DUKE OF EDINBURGH AWARD

This is a great scheme aimed at helping kids get the absolute most out of life!

There are four main aspects of the Duke of Edinburgh Award: gaining skills (a musical instrument, computers, cooking — the choice is yours); physical recreation (some sort of sport, which is, again, your choice); community service — helping people, the environment, or getting a first aid or life saving qualification; and also expeditions, such as bushwalking, canoeing, cycling, or overnight camping. You will first learn navigation and bushcraft skills and then go on several expeditions. There are three levels of awards — bronze, silver and gold.

Every kid I've known who has done it has found that at least some aspect of it is fun, challenging and incredibly rewarding — and it has led them into areas that they wouldn't have gone otherwise.

You can do the Duke of Edinburgh Award through your school or youth group, but if your school isn't involved and you don't belong to a youth group, then you can be a 'lone participant'.

There are branches in each state — look up Duke of Edinburgh Award in your local phone book (*White Pages*), or look up their website on: http://dukeofed.org.au. Each state has their own website and you will find links to them on the national website.

POLICE YOUTH CLUBS

Don't EVER feel that Police Youth Clubs will be a cross between school and a Gestapo holiday camp. They are usually anything but. They are run by people who are actually extremely interested in the courses they run and who are very, very unlikely to patronise you.

There is a heavy emphasis on macho stuff (excuse my bias — I'm female and middle-aged remember); sweat and martial arts, as well as stuff like mountain cycling, rock climbing, and abseiling, as well as anything from rock music or brass bands to bicycle education programs.

There are Police Youth Clubs in all capital cities and most major country areas, but the range of stuff they do varies enormously, depending on who happens to be stationed in that area, what the local kids are interested in, and how many other volunteers they can persuade to join.

No matter what you are interested in, it's worth giving them a buzz, just in case there's something that tickles your fancy. If there is something you are definitely interested in, they are good people to approach to see if they can organise anything along that line for you — you may be really surprised how much they will get into it with you.

Call your local police to see what's going on in your area.

(P.S. Police are actually friendly and approachable, as long as you don't happen to be robbing a bank, or look like you are planning to mug toddlers for their iceblocks. Most police joined the force because they *like* helping people.)

OUTWARD BOUND

Outward Bound was founded in 1941 to train young British seamen to cope in demanding circumstances. Now it's the largest professional, non-profit organisation involved in outdoor education and personal development in the world.

Outward Bound staff are well-trained and the courses are carefully selected to appeal to a wide range of age groups and abilities. Yes, there is an element of risk in most of their courses but that's the whole point — to challenge yourself so that you see what you are capable of — and to learn the discipline to minimise the risk.

There are too many courses to list here (including ones for adults) but a few of them include 7- and 8-day adventure courses for kids aged between 12 and 16 — either pack and paddle courses, or cross-country snow-skiing expeditions. There are also advanced adventures for reasonably experienced participants aged between 14 and 16; and family courses that involve things like scaling down an eighty foot caving ladder, sleeping in the outback, or spending 4 days on a 100-foot schooner.

There are also specially tailored courses for those with disabilities.

Outward Bound prices are kept as low as possible, and there are scholarships for those who aren't able to pay for themselves. This year's prices (1999–2000) range from $445 and upwards, for an eight-day adventure. There are courses all around Australia and overseas, and Outward Bound also organises central pick-up points that you can get to by public transport.

If you are feeling even remotely bored, it's well worth having a look at what Outward Bound can offer you.

Look up their website at: http://www.outwardbound. com.au or give them a call (it's free!) on 1800 267 999.

NORTHERN TERRITORY JUNIOR
RANGERS

Northern Territory Junior Rangers need to be 9 to 14 years old. The programme runs between March and October every year, and there are lectures and hands-on activities about all aspects of the environment — wetlands, weather, wildlife etc. There are also guest lecturers, family nights and excursions and members also get a free magazine, uniform, hat and shirt.

What will it cost?

Free!

Contact the Northern Territory Parks and Wildlife on (08) 8999 4565 or look them up on: http://www.nt.gov.au/paw

NORTHERN TERRITORY JUNIOR
POLICE RANGERS

This is a fantastic programme. You join up at the end of year 7, and it runs for three years.

In the first year you study everything from canoeing to navigation — basically, all the bush survival skills you might need.

In the second year you study these skills in even greater depth, including excursions out in the bush to really test your skills.

In the third year you study leadership and help take the younger members out into the bush.

What will it cost?

$250 a year, plus $30 for a uniform, shirt and cap.

Contact the Northern Territory Police Junior Ranger section on (08) 8922 3530, or look them up on the web at: http://www.nt.gov.au/pfes

LEADERSHIP WESTERN AUSTRALIA

This is a great programme set up to train tomorrow's leaders. You will do all sorts of leadership training, plus lots of hands-on stuff too. The courses are based in many areas around the state, and you will need to be 15 or over, and have a real interest in leadership, whether it is as part of your community, in business or government, or in youth groups.

To find out more, phone (08) 9476 2000, or send them a fax on (08) 9322 6544, or send an e-mail to: look@leadershipwa.com.au or visit the Leadership Western Australia website on: http://www.leadershipwa.com.au

YOUTH HOSTELS (Y.H.A.)

There are Youth Hostels all over Australia — in fact over much of the world. If you want a cheap, safe place to stay in a city, or at the beach (or loads of other places) it's worth joining the Y.H.A. (No, you don't have to be a kid to be a member — I just met a 94-year-old woman who has been Youth Hosteling all over North America with her great grand-daughter.) You can take your whole family youth hosteling! (Well, except the dog!) While the accommodation is pretty basic, it is always clean, convenient, friendly and very, very cheap. Membership costs $47 and the annual fee is $18. Kids pay $14.95 — or nothing if they have a parent who is a member. Then, when you travel, you pay between $10–$35 a night to stay in the hostel, which is incredible value for a room at the beach or in a capital city.

You can also stay at Youth Hostels if you are not a member, but you have to pay a premium rate that converts to membership after two nights.

The facilities at Youth Hostels can vary — they often have twin rooms or dormitories, and sometimes they have cheap cafeteria food, games rooms, TV lounges, cheap Internet access and swimming pools. (Just don't expect all of these things at any one of them!)

We had a Youth Hostel down the road from us for a few years, and we often met long-distance cyclists who were cycling all around Australia and staying at Youth Hostels about twice a week instead of camping, so they could have a hot shower, a comfortable bed, and do their washing (this is actually an incredibly cheap way to see Australia — and you really do see it, instead of being stuffed up in a car or bus)!

Look up 'Youth Hostels' in your phone book to enquire about membership.

HOLIDAY PROGRAMMES

School

Your school is probably the best place to find out about holiday programmes, because most holiday programmes send out all their information to schools.

Most of the time the schools pass this on to kids, but sometimes they have too much going on to get round to it, or they don't think that anyone would be interested, so it's worthwhile asking, 'Hey, are there any school holiday programmes on anywhere?' if, towards the end of term, no one has said anything yet.

Your school will also have details of holiday courses for kids interested in science, photography, computers, maths, writing workshops, pottery, etc. (If you're interested in ANYTHING there's probably a course about it somewhere.) Often no one will mention these because there are just too many to mention, if you see what I mean, but if you tell your teacher that you are really interested in doing extra work in a particular subject, they will probably look out for a course for you.

Museums

Largish museums (i.e. in capital cities and regional centres) often have school holiday programmes, or at least a school holiday display that might be worth exploring for half a day or so. It's worth giving them a ring. Even the small, local museums may have something on.

YMCA

The YMCA (in all capital cities) runs a wide range of holiday programmes, from the sort of activities where kids are booked in for the entire holidays while their parents are working (and the organisers try to come up with something new to entertain them every day) to specialist camps or day-excursions in mountain biking, bushwalking, and skiing. The YMCA also runs school holiday workshops in things like rollerblading, bicycle maintenance and so on. It's well worth giving them a ring to see what they have got on — and if there is something that you are particularly interested in that you can't do elsewhere, it's also worthwhile having a chat to them to see if they have anyone who can organise something for you — especially if you have a mob of friends who are interested too. (Of course, the more people it will appeal to, the more chance you have of convincing people to get it off the ground!)

Look up 'YMCA' in the *White Pages* of your local phone book.

National Parks

The various state national parks and wildlife services (each with slightly different titles) all run holiday programmes of varying levels of accessibility and sophistication.

Some require you to bring your own adult; others are organised for kids alone. Ring your local N.P.W.S. (or equivalent) office and enquire about holiday programmes. Some are extremely popular, so don't ring in the second week of the holidays or most of the spots will be taken. If you are going interstate for the holidays, then ring ahead of time and ask for information of forthcoming events.

Outward Bound

See Outward Bound on page 185 — there is always a wide range of challenging outdoor activity courses for all age groups.

Police Youth Clubs

See Police Youth Clubs on page 184. Police Youth Clubs often run day- or week-long excursions, ranging from skiing to sailing, mountain bicycling and camping — as well as their regular, year-round activities.

Libraries

Many libraries organise school holiday programmes — mostly involved with books (either reading or writing them), but sometimes there will be storytelling, drama classes, or computer courses. It's worth giving your local library a ring just to see if they have got anything planned and if they haven't, you might just get them thinking.

Large libraries usually have greater resources for holiday programmes than smaller ones — so if there is a state or regional library within easy travelling distance, then it's worth giving them a ring too.

THINGS TO GET YOUR SCHOOL TO DO

➤ Take an adventure holiday excursion — pay for a qualified guide to show you how to abseil, take you long-distance cycling, snowshoeing, or sea kayaking. Okay, it won't be for everyone, but for those that want to go, it will be an experience you will never forget.

(P.S. It's much cheaper to do all these things if you have a large group of you.)

➤ See if your school will allow you to have an overnight camp on the oval.

➤ Get your school to join WWOOF, then contact the host farms to find one who would be prepared to take a group of you, and a teacher and parent or two, to learn something about farming, growing your own fruit and veg, building a mudbrick wall, or operating your own power system.

➤ Get your school to subscribe to *Scientriffic*, *Double Helix*, or join the Dinosaur Club.

➤ Write your own book and use your school computers to print and publish it. (You could ask local businesses if they will sponsor it to help cover the paper costs, but if your parents and friends buy copies, that may pay for it anyway.) Or you could put it on the Internet.

➤ Join SETI so that your school can search for aliens.

➤ Make your next school excursion a treasure-hunting one — to find opals or flakes of gold.

➤ Get a school team together to break a world record in chocolate crackle-making (or something else). Get people to sponsor you to raise money for an adventure holiday.

➤ Raise native seedlings at your school to help revegetate eroded or salty areas.

➤ Record oral history on tape recorders.

➤ Organise a community art project for your local area, or a graffiti wall for your school.

➤ Organise a half-hour, monthly programme for your local FM community radio station.

NOTE TO PARENTS AND TEACHERS

Some of the activities in this book are dangerous (though certainly not all of them). Some are very dangerous. Kids may get hurt and in rare cases even killed.

Nowadays we try to make everything as safe as possible for kids — and that's a good thing. But there's a real difference between a kid getting hurt because they don't wear a helmet, or because playground equipment was badly designed or repaired — silly needless accidents — and kids being allowed to test themselves, to push their physical and mental limits further and further, and be stronger and more powerful people — physically and mentally — because of it.

Humans need challenge. We need to learn to cope with challenge — and we need to feel the triumph of succeeding. Sometimes I desperately wish that my son preferred nice, safe video games to climbing mountains. But most of the time I'm glad for him. (And all of the time I'm proud.)